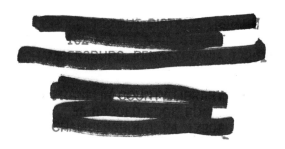

DAISIES ARE
FOREVER

DAISIES ARE FOREVER

•

SYDELL I. VOELLER

AVALON BOOKS
THOMAS BOUREGY AND COMPANY, INC.
401 LAFAYETTE STREET
NEW YORK, NEW YORK 10003

PRINTED IN THE UNITED STATES OF AMERICA
ON ACID-FREE PAPER
BY HADDON CRAFTSMEN, BLOOMSBURG, PENNSYLVANIA

c.1

Dedicated to my mother, Irene Lowell

Special thanks to:
Lee Oman,
Area Director, Oregon Department of Forestry

Chapter One

With loving strokes, April Heatherton brushed aside sun-parched fir needles from the old gravestone. Then she placed on it a bouquet of velvety, pealed, gold-brown daisies. Her mason jar made a perfect vase.

She stared down at the flat, three-cornered rock surrounded by white stakes and a simple cross made of mossy sticks. Dappled sunlight flickered through the towering Douglas firs as the July breeze whispered overhead.

Suddenly the rustling of footsteps close by startled her.

"Man alive! Look at those firs. They'll give

us at least twice the board feet we got up north," a husky voice proclaimed.

Heather's stomach dropped. Loggers . . . undoubtedly the ones from the neighboring town of Silton Pass nestled deep in the foothills of western Oregon. Most everyone in Wolf Hollow had heard the loggers would soon be clear-cutting the entire forest that blanketed North Creek Hill. The pit in her stomach grew deeper as realization took hold: her beloved hideaway—the unmarked pioneer grave—was alarmingly at risk. Why, in possibly a matter of mere weeks, one more tract of forest would lie in shambles, downed timber scattered like pickup sticks, the hillside carelessly gouged and barren!

Instinctively she drew back into the shadows, hoping the undergrowth would hide her. She would confront the loggers, but not yet, not until she'd had a chance to hear more of what they were saying.

Orion, her golden retriever, emitted a low, throaty growl.

"No, boy!" she commanded in a hoarse whisper, gripping the dog's leather collar in an effort to keep him close by her side. Though the aging dog was nearly deaf, he hadn't lost his keen sense of smell.

April peered cautiously around the side of

a stump, scarcely daring to breathe. She caught sight of two men squinting up at the mammoth evergreens.

The younger man, in his late twenties, she guessed, ran his hand through wheat-colored hair, pushing back an unruly lock from his forehead. He was clean shaven. His black T-shirt, cuffed at the sleeves, exposed his taunt, masculine biceps. "Yeah, what a loggin' show," he was saying. His voice was mellow, not at all gruff like his partner's.

"It's a cinch we'll get that contract," the older man put in. In his mid-fifties or so, he had a dark stubble of beard, wore a red checked shirt, denim jeans, and boots that came just below his knees. "Jake Thornburg told me most of the other companies were already backing out," he went on. "They're too small to hack the county's new land management requirements."

The first man turned to meet the other's gaze and broke into the most engaging grin April had ever seen. Even white teeth flashed against tanned skin. "I heard Thornburg say he planned to check out this hillside in the whirlybird today. I bet he'll like what he sees."

With that the two turned and began sauntering away.

"Wait! Stop! Destroying the forests is wrong!" April couldn't contain herself any longer. Her voice was filled with desperation as she quickly clipped Orion's leash to his collar, then started running after the men.

"What the . . ." The younger man stopped in midstride and tossed a look over his shoulder. "Well, looks as if we've got company," he drawled, his face splitting into a smile once again. His blue eyes flashed mischievously, his chin dimpled. "A bunny hugger, no less. A good-looking one too!"

April flinched at the sound of the all-too-familiar term, a name many of the locals had tagged the environmentalists. Orion growled again.

"Don't call me a bunny hugger!" she said hotly, new determination fueling her on. "I'm merely taking a stand! The timber here on North Creek Hill is one of the last old-growth forests in the entire coast range. In no time our ancient forests will be gone. And most of all, there's the . . ." She broke off abruptly, her sentence remained unfinished as she gestured helplessly back at the grave site, well out of view. How could she make them understand? They'd only accuse her of exaggerated female sentiment.

"We've heard all the arguments," the older

logger said. "Salvage the dwindling salmon, protect the spotted owl . . . the list goes on and on." He hitched his thumbs into his belt loops. "But you gotta know, lady, we're talkin' jobs here. Logging's been our bread and butter forever. And many of us, we've got wives and young 'uns to feed."

"Yes, but it's high time to start thinking about our future and our vanishing natural resources!" She drew in a ragged breath. The issues were complicated and double sided, and April knew there were no easy answers. After all, the loggers were only doing what many of their fathers, and perhaps their father's fathers, had done.

"See ya later," the younger guy said, obviously eager to let the entire issue drop. He smiled again and winked. "And try not to tangle with too many bunnies. That goes for your dog also."

She felt her cheeks flush with indignation as she turned to leave. Bunny huggers indeed! Who had ever come up with such a stupid comparison? Well, one thing she knew for sure. She must—no matter what—protect the unmarked grave of the pioneer woman and the beauty of the surrounding woodland.

This 100 acres of Ramult County forest bordered the land where her grandparents had built a home and planted a filbert orchard nearly a half century earlier. After April's parents were killed in a motorcycle accident when she was two, her grandparents raised her. Years later, April came to inherit the two-story clapboard house and surrounding property.

Ever since she'd been a small child, April loved to steal away farther into the woods on North Creek Hill to her own special retreat, a place where she was free to daydream, write poetry, and muse about nothing in particular.

Some of her friends had had their tree houses. Others found their special places in musty old attics. But every chance possible, April always returned to the pioneer woman's grave.

In summertime, she'd always bring bouquets of wild flowers from the neighboring meadow. In early autumn, she would gather succulent golden chanterelle mushrooms that grew in the cool, mossy shade. Come winter, usually empty handed, she'd brush away the brown parched leaves from the grave site, much as she'd just whisked away the sweetly scented fir needles.

Often Grandmother would accompany April there and tell her stories about the forests and animals, plus the settlers who had journeyed on the Oregon Trail. Gram had always held fast to a solemn reverence for the natural earth and her belief in a simple way of life.

As April grew to be a young woman, she pursued her teaching career, with a double major in biology and American history. What better way to pass on the ideals that bonded the past and the present, she'd decided. What better way to honor everything the unknown pioneer woman exemplified.

April turned and began trudging toward home while Orion trotted close by her side. A blue jay shrieked, sassing a crow. Breathing in the woodsy smells, she felt the tension flow from her body. She glanced at the sun as it slanted over the crest of the hill. Shadows were falling, making the dense slopes appear even darker. A bluish haze hung over them. Truly it was the most peaceful place on the entire earth, she thought dreamily.

A familiar beeping sound from the pager she wore on her belt loop jolted her from her reverie. She peered down at the screen and read, "A reminder for all Wolf Hollow fire department personnel: tonight's practice burn will begin promptly at 1900 hours. Business meeting will follow."

At the beginning of the summer, shortly after her twenty-sixth birthday, April had successfully completed her volunteer firefighter's training and claimed the distinction of being the second woman in the history of Wolf Hollow to have done so. Her best friend, Donna Walgren, had been the first.

April quickened her pace, then came to the first fork in the trail. The firs gave way to sparse groves of madronas, then the open meadow. The late afternoon sun sweltered unmercifully now, and perspiration ran down her face in rivulets. Pausing to lift her long auburn hair, she allowed the faint breeze to fan her neck and face.

She heard the babbling of North Creek, about fifty feet away, at the same time thinking that the sound should be much noisier, not a mere babble. The water levels in local creeks and streams had dropped significantly due to the recent near-drought conditions. *Oh, if only it would rain,* she thought. The rains of fall and winter typically kept the western Oregon forests lush and green.

In the distance the drone of a helicopter grew louder, drowning out the sounds of the creek. She jerked her head back, shading her eyes with her hand while the copter hovered like a giant mosquito above the treetops.

Fresh fear sprang inside of her. The whirly-bird! The helicopter the loggers had been talking about! Yes, it was definitely going to happen: soon they'd be clear-cutting North Creek Hill.

With a whir of silvery blades, the copter lowered momentarily, long enough for her to read the inscription on its side: JOHNSON BROTHERS LOGGING. Then, almost as quickly as it had appeared, the copter lifted and vanished over the next rise.

The ringing of the phone interrupted April's reading. After a longer-than-usual fire drill and a refreshing bubble bath, she'd curled up in her favorite chair to relax with a good book. The phone rang again and she jumped up to answer it, glancing at the brass clock on the fireplace mantel. It was nearly eleven. Who could be calling at this hour?

"I hope I didn't wake you," a lively voice spoke. Immediately April recognized the caller to be Donna.

"No, not at all. I was just reading a sci-fi novel and trying to wind down." She paused. "That was some killer fire drill tonight, wasn't it?" The firefighters had practiced on a condemned shack on the northwest side of town, and the battle to contain it had indeed posed a challenge.

"Yeah, I thought for sure we'd never get the fire out," Donna confessed. "But I didn't call for shop talk. At least not fire department shop talk. I'm thinking about next year at school."

"Oh? Aren't you a little early?"

"Not if you want to get a jump on things."

Both women taught at Wolf Hollow High School where they had also graduated eight years earlier. For April the balance of vocation with avocation seemed the perfect way to a well-ordered life—especially during her desperate attempts to heal from a broken romance the previous summer.

"So what's on your mind?" April prompted, then added, "Wait. Don't tell me." She tapped her index finger against the receiver. "You've probably come up with another brainstorm for a new cheerleading routine."

"No, silly. Though I'm admittedly gung-ho about my new job as cheering squad adviser, I don't plan to dream up any new routines till cheerleading camp later in August." Donna paused. "But I *have* come up with an idea to help you with your Pacific Northwest history classes this year. Interested?"

"Sure! What is it?"

"In today's paper—in case you missed it—there was an article about the logger's festival in Silton Pass this weekend. "The pioneer museum is free of charge with a general admission pass. There are supposed to be special displays in honor of the festival. Have you ever been there?"

April bit her lip. "Yes, but I'm afraid it was quite a while ago." She pushed back the image of the handsome young logger that Donna's suggestion had brought to her mind. The memory left her unsettled, with a vague, gnawing feeling. "I don't know, Donna," she continued. "It's just—"

"There's something else too," her friend cut in. "If we spend the best part of Saturday milling about the logging festival, we might be able to do a little detective work as to what's going to happen on North Creek Hill. I'm sure it'll be a hot topic there." Donna lived on the outskirts of town and shared April's concern about the local environmental issues.

"I already know."

"You do? How?"

April briefed her on what she'd heard the two loggers talking about earlier that afternoon. "It sounds as if it's practically decided.

Johnson Brothers plans on winning the bid hands down."

"So it's going through—no matter what?"

"Yes, I'm afraid so. I'm trying to be reasonable about all of these clear-cutting issues," April went on, as if more for her own benefit than Donna's. She stared down at her burgundy-colored bathrobe. "But I still can't bear to see the land around the pioneer woman's grave stripped bare."

"Me too," Donna said. "If North Creek Hill really *does* go on the auction block as scheduled, then that old-growth forest is doomed for sure. But I have an idea." April could hear the enthusiasm return to her best friend's voice. "Let's not worry about *why* we're going to the festival, let's just go and have a good time. After all, it's the biggest event of the summer around here. It should be fun—and in my opinion, you need to lighten up a little."

"I'm already having fun. I love my teaching job, and getting accepted as a volunteer firefighter has added a whole new dimension to my life."

"I'm not talking jobs and volunteer work," Donna insisted. "I'm talking romance."

"Romance?"

"Exactly. Who knows? There's bound to be some handsome, available man on the loose at the logging festival. Obviously you'll never meet any at the fire station. All the guys there are married and have a parcel of kids—even the ones that once swore they'd always remain single."

"I don't need any more handsome men in my life. Men only cause trouble. Especially men like Eric." April gripped the receiver more tightly as visions of Eric Mendelson paraded through her mind.

She'd met him a little over one year ago while she was enrolled in graduate classes at the university about an hour's drive away. Eric, who'd taken a three-month leave from Arrowtek, a successful computer company, met her every afternoon in the student commons to study together over double lattes.

His suave good looks, dry sense of humor, and preoccupation with details had fascinated April from the first moment they'd met. In no time, she'd fallen hopelessly in love with Eric—only to soon learn her love would go unrequited.

The sound of Donna speaking jerked April's attention back. "Maybe you think that about men, but I don't agree," she was saying.

"Huh?"

"I said I don't agree with your opinion about men. At least not *all* men . . ."

April's focus was right on target now. "Just because you're sporting the half-carat diamond engagement ring Travis gave at Christmastime doesn't mean romance is the answer for everyone," she insisted.

Donna chuckled. "Don't be jaded."

"Jaded? How else do you expect me to act when the only man I've ever loved turned out to be so wrong for me?"

"Didn't I warn you?" Donna answered April's question with one of her own. "Didn't I keep pointing out that Eric was a total computer junkie? And what about those hiking and camping trips that you ended up going on alone?"

"I know. Don't remind me. I guess I was too blinded by love to see that then."

"Yes, you were. And you were also too blind to see that Eric wasn't the least willing to compromise."

"That is, till the night he arrived on my doorstep and announced he'd found someone more compatible," April reminded her. "Boy, did I ever wake up then!"

"And now it's time to move on," Donna said with a mixture of sympathy and pragmatic realism. "It's time to put all that behind you."

She paused. "So what about the timber carnival? Will you go with me?"

"On one condition."

"What?"

"I'll go only in the name of research, pure and simple. I have absolutely no intentions of looking for a man. Understood?"

"Certainly."

Something in Donna's tone told April that her friend was only placating her.

"Hurry, April! The show's almost begun," Donna shouted over her shoulder.

April sprinted to keep up. "Wait! I'm coming." Together the two women pushed their way through the crush of people pressing toward the ticket gate. From the edge of the parking lot where the carnival rides were set up, organ grinder music pulsed through the speakers.

"Let's shoot for front-row seats," Donna said after April had caught up. She dug into her fanny pack for her wallet while April did the same.

Minutes later they ascended the bleachers that overlooked a man-made lake and sat down next to a lady who was munching popcorn.

"Ah! We made it!" April exclaimed, scanning the quickly filling seats.

Settling back, her thoughts drifted to their drive to Silton Pass. Donna had suggested they take her new white Accord and follow the scenic route that paralleled the busy interstate. They'd wended their way past old railroad trestles that bridged tree-carpeted ravines, the millpond jammed with floating logs, and sparkling Lost Lake nestled at the base of the foothills. Finally they arrived at the sprawling city park where the carnival was in full swing.

April gazed about at the other spectators, taking in their excited chatter, their smiles of anticipation. Parents with toddlers, grade-school children, and teenagers lined the bleachers. White-haired senior citizens looked on expectantly.

April recognized several of the folks, and as her gaze met theirs, she exchanged friendly hellos. Some were former students, the others, merchants and neighbors at Wolf Hollow. Yes, without a doubt, the light-hearted ambience was infectious, she decided. Maybe Donna had been right about her needing this day.

The rippling of applause interrupted her thoughts as the mayor of Silton Pass took his place on a small, portable platform. Welcoming the crowd, he delivered a brief history of the timber carnival. Then he introduced a middle-aged man by the name of Harvey Rawlings.

After giving a few more words of welcome, the man reached for a shiny rifle. With a sweep of his arm, he aimed the muzzle at a tall fir that stretched up from the lake shore. A shot reverberated in April's ears as the top of the tree ripped free, crashing to the ground.

The cheers from the crowd grew louder.

"Ladies and gentlemen, welcome to Silton Pass, Oregon. I, Harvey B. Rawlings, proudly launch the most spectacular timber carnival in the history of mankind!" he hollered into the microphone.

People whistled and stomped their feet.

"How'd he do that?" April asked Donna.

"The program says the tree was wired ahead of time with explosives."

"Oh." April chuckled. "I guess I've been too busy gawking to read the fine print."

As a souped-up chain saw began to whine, scattering wood splinters in every direction, April turned her attention to the opening event, the hot power saw competition, and settled back to watch.

The hour passed quickly. As one contest gave way to the next, April's fascination mounted. Men with ropes secured around their waists and wearing high-top boots ascended trees stripped of branches.

In minutes they were cutting through the tops with handsaws. Others chopped at standing log blocks until the first severed pieces toppled down. When it was time for the ax-throwing contest, Mr. Rawlings told the audience it was often considered the logger's oldest sport.

The sun radiated down, warming April's shoulders and back. From somewhere behind the bleachers, the aroma of buttery popcorn and barbecued beef wafted on a gentle breeze. The rainbow of sights, sounds, and delicious aromas everywhere about her made April feel relaxed and carefree.

Next came the men's log-rolling event on the lake. As the first two contestants emerged onto the dock, April's jaw dropped. She strained to see better, certain one of them was the young blond logger she'd talked to on North Creek Hill. He ambled closer.

Yes, that *had* to be him, she decided. There was no mistaking it. Today his face and arms were more deeply tanned, contrasting with his navy blue tank top and white shorts as he strode, surefooted, to the edge of the dock. His well-formed muscles were taut and glistening.

"Wow! Look at that guy!" Donna breathed. "What a hunk!"

April swallowed hard in an effort to suppress the shivers of attraction pressing down on her. "Stop that!" she teased. "You're *engaged,* remember?"

"Of course I remember. And believe me, in my estimation, no one could compare to Travis. But that doesn't mean I can't still appreciate the competition, does it?"

April laughed. "No, I suppose not." She struggled to maintain an indifferent air. If she was showing any outward signs of her own awareness of the guy's masculine good looks, she must make certain not to let it show. No point giving her overly eager friend reason for any false hope.

The sound of the emcee's rising voice sliced through April's reflection. "The first contestant for the log-rolling contest is Matt Spencer from Silton Pass!"

Matt, April thought. *Matt Spencer.* Carefully she turned the name over in her mind, deciding it had a nice down-to-earth ring. Yes, it matched him well. Earthy and rugged in a laid-back, chivalrous sort of way—despite the maddening fact he'd called her a bunny hugger. At the memory, she felt the heat rise to her face. Funny that it still bothered her so. After all the razzing she endured from the guys at the fire station, she should be accustomed to it by now.

Precariously Matt balanced himself on the floating log a few feet from his opponent, a well-built man with a bushy red beard. The water below them rippled, catching glimmers of noonday sunlight.

After Harvey Rawlings introduced the other competitor, he explained the rules: "Two out of three falls will decide a match," he announced into the public address system. "May the best man win!"

The two men started running in place on top of the log, whirling it faster and faster. April stared, transfixed. After what seemed an eternity, the bearded man lunged into the lake, sending up a fountain of white spray.

The audience roared with laughter, clapping their hands. Soon the contestants were at it again.

Someone from off to the side cheered. "Come on, Spencer! You can do it! Go for it!"

April held her breath. Two, three, four more minutes ticked by. Suddenly it appeared Matt was losing his balance. He threw his hands out to his side in an attempt to regain it, but it was too late. In a flash, he hit the water. More cheers and catcalls exploded all about.

In no time the two men were back on the log, spinning it again like a toy top. "One minute to go!" the emcee bellowed into the speaker.

A frown crossed Matt's face as he began to falter. Then he quickly righted himself, teetering once again on the slippery wet log before he geared back into motion. The seconds seemed to stand still. The bearded man wavered, arms flailing, and plunged into the water.

The spectators stamped their feet and yelled.

"It's a match!" Harvey Rawlings exclaimed. "The winner is Matt Spencer!"

Matt let out a whoop, jumped into the water, and swam to the dock. When he emerged over the side, he flashed a grin, then raised his hands in a sign of victory while the crowd continued to cheer.

Sitting on the edge of her seat, April clapped so vigorously her palms began to sting. "Way to go, Matt!" she yelled at the top of her lungs, purposefully ignoring Donna's open-mouthed stare. "I knew you could do it!"

He looked in her direction, his gaze no longer sweeping the crowd. Their eyes locked. His grin widened.

For an immeasurable moment, he just kept staring at her as if the others in the bleachers no longer existed.

Chapter Two

"Allemande left with the corner maid, do-se-do your babe, men star by the left, you roll it once around the set." The square dancers moved in a kaleidoscope of color, the women's full, bright skirts bouncing gently to the music. Even a boy and girl about age eight, April guessed, were weaving fluidity in and out the moving circle.

After the show, April and Donna had agreed to go their separate ways. Donna, who said she was so hungry she could eat anything that didn't eat her first, headed for the barbecue beef concession; April was curious about the historical museum. They agreed to meet back near the bleachers in two hours.

23

On the way there, at the edge of the parking lot, April paused to watch the dancers. Still thinking about Matt, she glanced over her shoulder. Was he somewhere close by? Had his questioning look from back on the dock been purely incidental? Or had he remembered every bit as distinctively as she their meeting on North Creek Hill?

While part of her longed to talk with him again, the other part warned to avoid him at all cost. Yes, someone like Matt Spencer, whose goals clashed so acutely with hers, indeed spelled trouble. No way would she ever again fall for a man who was so wrong for her.

The sound of the lively music pulled her back to the present. The caller's voice droned above the harmonizing twang of the guitars and banjos. Momentarily forgetting her discomforting thoughts, she crossed her arms over her chest, smiled, and nodded her head to the beat. If someone would've tapped her on the shoulder right then and invited her to join in, she would've been tempted—though she hadn't square-danced since the sixth grade.

At last she tore herself away from the music and crossed the lawn to the entrance of the museum where a petite lady dressed in a

cornflower blue pioneer dress and white bonnet handed her a brochure. "Welcome to the
historical museum." She smiled. "If you have
any questions, feel free to ask me or any
other of our volunteers."

"Thank you." April returned her smile as
she accepted the brochure and stepped inside. "I teach U.S. history at Wolf Hollow
High School and I'm looking for new project
ideas," she explained.

"I'm so glad to hear that." The woman
pointed toward the back of the anteroom
where they were standing. "For starters, perhaps the display of the old-time logging
equipment might interest you."

"Yes, I think it will. Thanks again."

The first thing she noticed was a machine
with thick cables wound inside enormous
drums. The sign beneath it said it was a donkey engine that was powered by steam and
used to drag the logs out of the woods. Long
jagged-tooth saws were mounted on a backdrop behind the donkey engine.

She moved on to a glass showcase, debat-
ing what would best catch her students'
attention. She peered inside at an old-
fashioned christening gown with rows of lace,
yellowed with age, a pair of booties, and a
muslin bonnet. About a half-dozen frayed

black-and-white photographs lay beneath the baby garments. In one picture, a logging family sat in front of their homestead, built beneath a thick canopy of evergreens. Three stern-looking, bearded men squinted back at the camera, and nearby a pretty woman with dark hair knotted in a loose bun held a cherubic baby wearing the christening garb. The picture was dated 1886.

Spellbound, April reflected—as she had so many times in the past—on what it had been like raising a family with nothing but wilderness and hardship all about. The dangers. The plagues. The stricken babies and children. The pioneer women who'd journeyed on the Oregon Trail had always taken special interest in the grave sites they'd found along the way. And many had remained unmarked, just like the unmarked grave on North Creek Hill.

Perhaps a skit, a reenactment of pioneer days, would spark her students' creativity, April decided as she turned her thoughts back to the coming fall. The high school in Wolf Hollow was known for its strong interest in drama, and surely the costumes wouldn't be too difficult to find or make.

She peered again at the photos in the showcase. Her fascination grew as teams of oxen lumbering across the skid roads of early logging days and rustic logging camps marched before her.

"Pretty amazing, huh?"

She looked up and blinked twice. Matt Spencer was standing alongside of her, eyeing her with obvious interest.

"Uh . . . yes," she stammered. Her stomach turned over. "I . . . I was so absorbed in it all, I didn't realize anyone else was here looking too." She forced herself to face him squarely. He was wearing a clean white T-shirt, cutoff jeans, and a funky pair of red, white, and blue suspenders—undoubtedly in celebration of the annual logging event.

The corners of his blue eyes crinkled as his gaze locked with hers. "I've been known to single out pretty young women a time or two."

"Oh—" She took two steps back, feeling like a flustered schoolgirl at a loss as to what to say. Had he purposely followed her here? Was there some connection with the way he had been looking at her from the dock and the way he was looking at her this very moment?

"Don't I know you from somewhere?" he asked. His eyes glinted with amusement while he waited for her reply.

"Yes. We met on North Creek Hill one afternoon last week. Well, I guess I should say, we *sort of* met." She hesitated, gritting her teeth. "I'm the bunny hugger, remember?"

He tossed back his head and laughed, an easy, rumbling sound that made her feel all warm inside. "Of course! How could I forget?" He offered his hand. "Matt Spencer," he said.

She took it. "Yes. Hello." His grip was firm, strong, and strangely disarming. "I'm April. April Heatherton."

"The pleasure's mine." Sobering, he nodded to the nearest photo. "Interested in a little history lesson?"

"Uh . . . sure."

"That baby was my great-grandmother on my dad's side. The woman holding her was my great-great-grandmother. I can't remember their names, but I think they're recorded in our family Bible."

"No kidding?"

"Yep. Scout's honor."

"So one of those men must be your great-great-grandfather too," she said evenly.

"Yeah, the one on the far left." He jerked his head to one side, causing a lock of blond hair to tumble across his forehead. "He's the only man who isn't wearing a hat."

"What a handsome-looking family," she

said sincerely while struggling to remain matter of fact. Fresh emotions somersaulted inside of her. She couldn't help but make the association with his own rugged good looks. "Speaking of history lessons, I teach high school history," she added, as if to imply that her interest in what they were discussing was merely professional.

"A teacher, huh?" He turned and looked at her again, his brows raised, another smile tugging at the corner of his mouth. "You don't look much older than a teenybopper yourself."

"I've been teaching four years now, thank you," she replied in a huff. "And I'm the second woman in the entire history of Wolf Hollow to be accepted as a volunteer firefighter."

"Wow!" He rocked back on his heels and, snapping his suspenders, laughed. "And I bet you can be a fiery little devil too, when you set your mind to it."

"I stand up for what I believe in, if that's what you mean."

"Good." He winked broadly. "By the way, what did you think of the logging show?"

"The competition, you mean?"

"Yep."

"It was terrific!" She ventured a smile,

backing off some from her previous defensive posture. Why did this man rile her so?

"The proceeds go to a good cause," he explained. "The money is kept in a kitty for whenever a busted-up logger needs it. Logging families have a way of looking out for each other," he added with a hint of pride in his voice.

April nodded. "Congratulations on winning the men's log-rolling contest," she told him. The crowded museum was growing uncomfortably warmer by the minute. A steady stream of air from an overhead fan cooled her.

"Thanks," Matt replied. "I have to admit, falling in the drink was a welcome relief. I can't remember when it's ever been so blasted hot, this time in July."

"You should've just kept on your wet clothes," she commented levelly. "At least you would've stayed cooler for a little while."

She allowed her gaze to drift to his broad chest and couldn't help noticing how his T-shirt strained across it. Quickly she tore her eyes away. He'd look divine, no matter *what* condition his clothes were in.

"You read me right," he agreed with a quick laugh. "Hanging loose is definitely my style." He hesitated, eyeing her steadily.

"But I wasn't sure what you'd think about that. I mean, turning up in wet clothes isn't exactly the . . . the"—he thought for a moment—"the best way to meet a lady."

"Oh?" She angled him a look. "This was a deliberate plan, you catching up with me?"

His blue eyes, flecked with brown, laughed down at her. "Might say so."

She dragged in a steadying breath, wracking her mind for a quick change of subject. "Are you going to take part in any other contests today?" she asked.

"I was supposed to have competed in the chokersetter's event, but I didn't sign up in time." He paused, pursing his lips. "During the time I've been working with Johnson Brothers—which is about a year or two longer than you've been teaching, I suspect—I've actually done more chokersetting than log rolling."

She laughed. "Chokersetting. That term has always fascinated me. Sounds like something out of an Agatha Christie novel."

He laughed too. "I suppose so. As you might already know, a chokersetter is the guy who slips a special cable over the end of a cut tree. When the yarder, the one who hauls the logs to the landing, pulls it, the log must ride all the way through the woods without hanging up on anything, like old stumps and rocks."

"But why do they call it chokersetting?"

"Because when the yarder yanks on the log, the looped cable tightens in on the end of it like a noose."

"Oh, I get it." She hesitated. "So that's what you do in the woods? That's your job?" He was standing very near, and she caught the fresh, manly scent of his aftershave. New awareness shivered through her.

"Yep, that's it," he answered. He glanced about, fanning his face with his museum brochure. "I could go for a nice cool drink right now. How would you like to check out the concessions with me?"

"All right," she answered after a moment's pause. She glanced at her watch, then added, "Just as long as we don't have to go too far." There was still over a half an hour till she was due to meet Donna. So what would it hurt just this once, spending a little time with him? After today, she'd probably never see Matt Spencer again.

He cupped his hand beneath her elbow as they threaded their way back through the crowded building. Again his touch brought disturbing new sensations. April couldn't

help wondering at his nonchalant yet cour-
teous manner.

Outside, a cool breeze welcomed them. After he'd paid for two frosty sodas—despite
April's insistence she pay for her own—they
sat down on a vacant green slatted park
bench beneath the umbrellalike shade of a
towering willow.

"This is so much better," April said between eager sips. She yanked off her sandals
and plunged her toes into the tall, soft blades
of grass. From somewhere in the distance,
the sound of a fiddle tune drifted their way.
"Ah, much, much better," she added. She
turned to Matt and offered a polite smile. "So
tell me. Did you grow up in a family of loggers
like so many of the others around here? Is
that why you decided to work in the woods
too?"

He averted his gaze, looking somewhere
over her shoulder, as if deciding how to answer. "Yes and no. Yes, most of the men in
my family have been loggers. No, that's not
entirely why I decided to work in the woods."

"Meaning?"

"Meaning that while I was attending
Oregon State and majoring in engineering,
I discovered I would never be happy build-
ing big-city skyscrapers and bridges. So I

came back to Silton Pass and went to work for my father's logging company, Johnson Brothers."

"And you're happy now?" she asked. "It seems to me there's not much future in what you've come back to. You and I both know there's already a lot of displaced loggers."

"I'm very happy. And, like you, I fight for what I believe in. You've got to remember, there's more than one way to look at clear-cutting. It's not only economical, but it gives the best conditions for replanting Douglas fir and other evergreens that don't tolerate a lot of shade." He angled her a look. "And speaking of my future, I'm my father's only son. Some day when Dad's ready to hang up his boots, I'll probably take over the business. That is, if it still exists," he added darkly.

She bit her lip, puzzling over how he could choose to continue endangering the ancient forests, the wildlife.

He must've sensed her hesitation, for suddenly his eyebrows knit together. "There's something you need to know. I'm not totally opposed to newer harvesting practices, like partial cuts and helicopter logging. I'm not necessarily against *all* the new government regulations either."

"For instance?"

"For instance, I agree that in some cases it might be better to practice selective harvesting. I like the idea of leaving trees in which birds and other small animals can live—especially in the areas where endangered species, like the marbled murrelet, have been known to nest."

"Good! Now you're finally talking—"

"Hold on," he cautioned, cutting her off. "You seem to be forgetting one thing."

"Oh? What?"

"North Creek Hill is *not* one of these areas. So far, no one has proved any endangered birds exist there."

"But don't you see, Matt? Even the environmentalists and the Forest Service can't agree. While one side insists that finding physical evidence such as an eggshell or a nest is sufficient proof, the other side demands more scientific protocols."

"Scientific protocols!" he snapped. "That's nothing but a lot of high-minded talk! Why, I bet even you don't really understand what that's supposed to mean."

The knot in her stomach seemed to be inching up to the base of her throat. She sensed Matt felt pulled in two directions, wanting to continue logging in the way his father had, while at the same time reconciling himself with the future.

Truth was, she felt ambivalent also, perhaps even more so now that she and Matt had become better acquainted. Yet as far as the pioneer woman's grave was concerned, one fact remained. April was determined to protect it, no matter what the cost.

"Look, I know you don't fully understand." Matt touched her shoulder again. This time his hand lingered a little too long. "But I have a suggestion."

"Oh?" She pulled back.

"There's a dance tonight at the armory across the street, starting at eight. Billy Murton and the Horseshoe Mountaineers. I'll introduce you to my dad and some of the other guys too. Good, hard-working family men, I might add. Maybe we can prove to you we're not the insensitive jerks you seem to think we are."

"Why not meet them right now?" she asked. She held his gaze, struggling to ignore the edge in his voice.

"Dad had to go into town to take care of some business. He left right after the log-rolling contest. He'll be back later, though, in time for the dance. And it should be a good one. It always is."

She shook her head, heeding the voice inside her that cautioned against prolonging their time together any further. "No thanks. Besides, I believe I've already met your father. Weren't you with him on North Creek Hill? That man—whoever he was—looked a lot like you."

"Yep, that was Dad. But I hardly call that a real meeting."

"Perhaps not. But it's not as if I've never met a logger before and need to be enlightened. I've grown up around loggers all my life. Everyone who lives here has."

"But I bet your growing-up years were long before you became a radical."

"I'm not a radical," she insisted. "I prefer to express my views in subtle ways. I have a personal interest in North Creek Hill, a reason for—"

"And right now, so do we!" His blue eyes flared with sudden anger. "Winning that contract means big bucks, our very lifeblood."

"So you see? There's no point trying to talk things out. You and your father and the other loggers too . . . we'd only remain at odds."

A long, cold silence stretched between them. "April?" he asked at last, his voice contrite.

"Yes?" She lifted her eyes to meet his.

"Do . . . do you think there's a chance we could ever agree?"

"I don't know."

The ghost of a smile touched his mouth. "There's one thing I do know for sure. I want to get to know you better."

A swell of confused feelings rose up inside of her. She raked her hand through her loose mane of auburn hair. "I don't think that's a good idea. Besides, I'm supposed to meet my friend back at the concession stands in exactly . . ." She broke off, glanced at her watch, then bounded to her feet. "Oh no! I'm already late!"

"Who's your friend?" he asked tightly.

"Donna Walgren, who teaches at the school where I do. We've been friends since before either of us can remember."

A wave of relief passed over his face. "Look, I'll make you a deal—"

"April, where have you been?" A shrill voice sliced through their conversation. It was Donna, sprinting from seemingly out of nowhere, her disheveled, short blond curls framing her freckled face. On the top of her head was perched a pair of dark-framed sunglasses.

"I've been looking all over for you!" Donna exclaimed. "Oops, sorry." Clapping her hand over her mouth, her eyes grew wide. She'd actually had the grace to blush. "Didn't mean to interrupt anything. I'll talk quick and disappear."

"Not necessary," Matt said reassuringly. "We were about to—"

"I just wanted to tell April that I called Travis at work today," Donna interrupted again, this time her eyes flickering appreciatively over Matt.

"Travis?" he asked.

"Yes. Travis Lagler. My fiancé."

"And you're Donna, I suppose?"

"Got it. April and I've been best friends practically since we were both cutting our first teeth."

"So I hear." He held out his hand. "Pleased to meet you, Donna. I'm Matt Spencer."

"I know." Donna's eyes sparkled with her unveiled admiration as she shook his hand. "I saw you win the log-rolling contest. You looked absolutely great."

"So what *about* Travis?" April was quick to divert Donna's attention away from Matt. "What did he say when you phoned him?" It wasn't that she didn't trust her best friend. She did. It was just that she had difficulty handling the twinge of jealousy she'd unexpectedly experienced.

"Travis is getting off early today," Donna answered. "He's a lineman with the phone company and darned good one too," she added for Matt's benefit.

"I'm sure," he answered levelly.

"Anyway," Donna continued, "Travis is going to come here in an hour. I happened to mention the dance at the armory tonight and he thought it sounded cool. April, you don't mind if we hang out till it starts, do you?"

"Uh . . . well." April's voice squeaked as she shot her friend a desperate look. "I don't know."

"That's exactly what April and I were talking about," Matt put in, dismissing April's last words. "The logger's stomp dance is always a blast. This year it's supposed to be better than ever."

"Then let's go!" Donna exclaimed.

"Yeah," Matt agreed. He gave April a long, speculative look and when she didn't object he added, "Meet me there at eight."

"All right." She met his gaze, squaring her shoulders. "All right, Matt. You win."

"Man in the moon, bright stars above, you know how much I need, someone to love." With a nasal twang, the guitar player crooned the popular country tune. Blue and red neon lights flashed from behind the refreshment bar while loud talking mingled with the beat of the music.

Matt peered through the crowded dance hall toward the large double doorway. He dragged in a ragged breath. It was almost half past eight and so far, no sign of April.

"Blast it!" Why was he becoming so edgy, so restless? He'd known plenty of women, and it had always been the same. Easy come, easy go. Yet somehow he suspected this time was different. For some crazy reason he couldn't get this lady out of his mind.

His thoughts raced on as he crossed his arms over his chest and leaned against the wall. The hard surface pressed against his back like a flat cold stone, matching the yawning coldness in the pit of his stomach. Maybe that's what it was, he reasoned. April *was* a lady, a real lady—though definitely not the white gloves and lace type. It hadn't taken him long to tell she was intelligent, spirited, and deeply caring, despite their differences. Women like that were hard to find.

But wait a minute! He jammed his hands into the pockets of his denim jacket and groaned. This was stupid! What was coming over him? He'd barely known her for a couple of hours and already he was getting all sappy. Well, whatever . . . all that mattered now was seeing her again.

The music ended, and a cacophony of laughter rose up about him. Elbowing his way through the crowd, he started across the spacious dance floor to the table where his father was sitting, swapping stories with a couple of his old cronies. "Stay put, Dad," he muttered under his breath, rehearsing what he'd say when he finally got there. "Don't pack it in early. Not yet."

If anyone could melt down the lady's preconceived notions, it had to be Dad.

Chapter Three

Inhaling a calming breath, April stepped inside the armory. The steady beat of the music and the harmonizing swells pulsed about her. She waited for her eyes to adjust to the semidarkness, then caught sight of the band on the opposite side of the dance floor.

The lead singer, a guy with a head of reddish curls and a close-cropped beard, was belting out a familiar song. Next to him stood a guitarist, a harmonica player, and a pretty blond woman who plunked away at a honky-tonk piano. The faint scent of beer drifted in from outside. Though the sale of liquor was prohibited inside the armory, a small beer garden had been set up not far from the main entrance.

Nervously April looked about. The place was packed! Where could Matt be? she wondered. Donna and Travis had already started dancing. Naturally, April thought, the song had to be one of Donna's many favorites. She'd insisted that her fiancé sweep her onto the dance floor the minute he'd arrived.

Squaring her shoulders and plastering a smile on her face, April slowly threaded her way through the crowd. If Matt had insisted she needed to meet his father, she intended to do that as quickly as possible, then put them both out of her mind. How did she ever let herself get talked into coming here in the first place?

Still, she felt a small catch at the back of her throat, a tiny spark deep inside of her at the thought of seeing Matt again. Witnessing Donna and Travis's happiness these past months had left her with a vague yearning deep inside, a reminder of what could have been a reality in her own life—if only she and Eric hadn't been so ill suited.

"Ah, there you are!"

She gave a start, then glanced up. Matt was smiling down into her eyes with that wicked gleam that already seemed deliciously inviting.

"Hi. You made it" was all she could manage.

"Hi yourself." He was still staring at her, the dimple in his chin deepening.

"They really jam them in here, don't they?" Her words came in a rush. "I . . . I was beginning to wonder how we'd ever find each other."

"It mattered to you?"

"I promised I'd come, didn't I?"

"Yes." He squared his jaw, the look in his blue eyes growing more intense.

"Where's your father?" she asked, glancing about.

Matt motioned across the armory. "Over by those tables. It looks as if he's chewing the fat with his old buddy Salty."

She peered through the semidarkness, but the tables were too far away to single out any particular face.

"I hope the numbers in here are in compliance with fire codes," she said, quirking a cautious eyebrow.

Matt looked amused. "No problem. I didn't tell you earlier, but I was part of the committee that planned this event. We covered all our bases."

"Good."

He caught her hand in his, hoping against all hope for a chance to start over with her. Yet somehow it seemed she was more defensive now than ever.

"Let's dance," he said.

"Let's not. According to you, we were supposed to hold some kind of all-important summit conference tonight," she said in a saucy tone. "I suggest we get on with it, Spencer."

He glanced in the direction where his father was sitting. "We will, but it'll have to wait. I see Dad and Salty heading outside right now."

"Oh, right. First you tell me that I should meet 'good old dad,' then suddenly the man turns up unavailable? What was this, Spencer, a setup?"

His steady look chided her for being impudent. "Of course not. I'm sure Dad's only leaving for a few minutes. He's a little hard of hearing, and loud noises always get to him."

"Too much exposure to all those deafening chain saws."

"Not necessarily." His eyes flashed with . . . with what? Determination, insult, challenge? "Let's dance," he said again.

She met his gaze, felt the firm grip of his hand. Her heart leaped, defying the instant warning that sprang to mind: *No! You're making a mistake! You'll regret this tomorrow!*

"All right." A sigh of defeat escaped her lips as he led her onto the dance floor.

The music had changed to a slow dance, and in only a moment he'd clasped her tightly against him as they molded together, swaying to the gentle rhythm. The warmth of him made her pulse race. He smelled of mint chewing gum and fresh air.

"I was afraid you might not show up tonight," he murmured into her ear, nudging her closer.

"It mattered to you?" she asked, pulling back, deliberately parroting what he'd said a few minutes earlier.

"You don't get off your high horse easily, do you?"

"Sorry." She inhaled another calming breath and silently counted to ten. What had come over her? Why was she so intent on this verbal sparring with Matt? All he had asked, for heaven's sake, was that she meet his father. Did her edginess have anything to do with the way his physical closeness was unraveling her?

"Travis told us he ran into road construction," she continued in a more civil tone. "It took him twice as long to get here as it should've and I'd promised Donna I'd hang out with her till he arrived."

"Oh."

She could feel the heat of his hand against her back. Suddenly she was heady and strangely breathless. Why, not even Eric had affected her this way. . . .

They danced on until intermission, and April was relieved when the time had finally arrived. Maybe now, for the rest of the evening, she could better maintain her distance from Matt—not only physically, but emotionally as well.

After chatting briefly with Donna and Travis, who appeared to be having a fabulous time, they excused themselves and wandered to the outermost edges of the dance floor. April turned to Matt. "Is your dad back yet?"

"I think so. Let's go find out for sure."

Hooking an arm around her waist, he led her toward a cluster of round tables where folks of all ages sat, laughing and talking.

"Dad, I'd like you to meet a friend of mine, April Heatherton," Matt announced. "April, my father, Abraham Spencer."

The older man's eyebrows rose in silent approval as he lumbered to his feet.

"Please! Please stay seated," April said, extending her hand.

Abraham Spencer's massive, rough palm engulfed hers. The man had intense blue eyes, much like Matt's. They studied her from beneath bushy gray brows.

"Sit down, my dear." He pulled out a chair for her. It screeched against the wooden floor, the sound punctuating the rising murmur about them.

"Thank you." She did as he'd indicated and offered him a tentative smile.

"Haven't I seen you around?" Abraham Spencer asked.

"Yes, this is the lady we met a few days ago up on North Creek Hill," Matt supplied, straddling a stool alongside of her.

"Hmm . . . April Heatherton," he said. He drawled the words like honey dripping off a spoon. "I must say, that's the most pleasant name I've heard in a long time. Makes me think of a spring mornin' filled with sunshine and flowers."

"Don't put too much stock in a name," Matt cut in with an exaggerated wink, which was clearly directed at his father. "This one's a real grizzly disguised as a toy panda."

"Now, Matthew," Abraham Spencer reprimanded playfully. "You think I haven't handled my share of grizzlies in my day?"

Heather felt the warmth flooding to her face. She darted a look at Matt, then pulled her gaze back to his father. What had Matt meant by "this one"? Well, whatever it was supposed to signify, at least she sensed a warm camaraderie between father and son.

"You from these parts, young lady?" Abraham Spencer asked.

"Uh-huh. Wolf Hollow. I grew up there, and a few years ago, came back to teach school."

"Nice little town. About one-quarter the size of Silton Pass, I think."

"Yes, a *very* nice little town. And most of the citizens would like to see it stay that way," she added pointedly.

The corners of his eyes crinkled in amusement, but then his expression grew sober. "Not long ago I found an injured fawn in the woods not far from Wolf Hollow. She'd apparently been hit by a car or logging truck."

"Poor thing," April said, momentarily letting down her guard. What would happen to the wildlife on North Creek Hill if the clear-cutting did indeed go through? she wondered.

Abraham Spencer narrowed his gaze in

recollection. "Well, this fawn had a real bad busted-up leg. At first I was going to finish her off with my rifle, but then I knew I couldn't do it—not with those soft big brown eyes staring at me so pitiful like."

As he talked, April took in his weathered skin, the heart-shaped tattoo on his lower arm, the flesh-colored hearing aid tucked unobtrusively behind one ear. Confusion washed over her. Somehow Abraham Spencer didn't quite match her first impressions of him that day in the woods, but she wasn't about to change her mind quite so soon.

"So what finally happened? Did the fawn make it okay?" she asked, reigning in her thoughts.

"Yes, my dear. But not until I'd first loaded her into my one-ton pickup and hauled her into Doc Crawson's animal hospital. He's been a vet in Silton Pass forever, you know. Anyway, I guess he thought I was some kind of a crazy man, tellin' him to take that deer and patch her all up. I told him I'd pay whatever was necessary to get the job done, but he said not to worry about the money. Yes sir, he doctored that critter and kept her there at the clinic for quite a while. Then, when he figured she was mended, he called me and I drove her back into the woods to let her go. What a day, seein' her boundin' back into the woods so graceful like." He gave a wan smile. "I guess my wife's love for wildlife sort of rubbed off on me."

"Yes. It's important we protect all our wildlife."

"And I agree, young lady—within reason." His voice was even, neither harsh nor judgmental.

She glanced over at Matt in hopes of catching some nonverbal cue about this exchange between his father and her. But Matt was just sitting there, arms folded, his long, muscular legs stretched out before him. His expression remained closed.

"So what's going to happen on North Creek Hill?" she asked without further preamble. Her eyes flitted from Matt to his father.

"Johnson Brothers is going to win that bid, that's what!" Matt jumped in.

"Our contract with the mill will be for that entire one hundred acres of timber," the older man added. "In fact, Harry Morton, the mill owner himself, was sitting here chatting with me a little while ago. Salty was here too. He's my right-hand man."

"So where is this . . . er . . . Mr. Morton now?" April asked, hoping she also might have an opportunity to talk with the man.

"He headed out early. Got to be at his desk first thing tomorrow."

"I see." April sighed. So far, it seemed she wasn't going to learn any more than she already knew about the timber auction.

Before she could ask any further questions, the music blasted again, this time louder than ever.

Abraham Spencer scowled, then fumbled with his hearing aid. "Dang that noise!" He darted first April, then Matt an apologetic glance. "You kids might as well go back out on the dance floor and kick up your heels. As for me, it's time to head home."

"I'm glad to have met you," April said. Despite the volatile topic they'd just barely touched upon, she couldn't deny her growing fascination with Matt's father.

He got to his feet. "The pleasure's all mine. I hope I'll see you sometime again."

"Yes"—she hesitated—"me too."

After Matt's father had left, Matt stood up and pulled her to her feet. "Let's head out for a little fresh air," he said.

She nodded in agreement as they crossed the large expanse to the front of the auditorium. By the main entrance, a group of men had convened, talking in loud, angry voices.

Two of them wore full beards and hair pulled back in single braids.

Matt clasped her hand, tossed an angry look at the men, then steered her clear of the brewing debate. His grip tightened.

"So these are the loggers, the hard-working family men you were trying to convince me would be here tonight," she commented dryly.

"I don't know *who* those characters are," he said with a growl. "Certainly not anyone *I* know." They passed by the ticket office, through the large foyer, then finally outside into the cool night air.

"It may be true that some loggers have a reputation for packing away lots of suds," Matt went on, apparently still mulling over what they'd just seen and heard. "We work hard, play hard, and we're proud of it. But the sad fact is, people often think loggers have big vests and small hats. It can take a long time to change old ideas."

"And I suppose I'm your first challenge," she said lightly. Crickets chirped from the field bordering the sprawling parking lot. From inside the armory, the moody sounds of steel guitars and drums wafted.

"First challenge?" He chuckled. "Well, now

that you've put it that way . . ." His voice trailed.

"Trust me, Matt," she said, her voice turning sincere. "In spite of everything I've said, I really do want to be open-minded." She wasn't sure exactly why his trust was so important to her right then, but it was.

"And if I *do* trust . . ." He stopped midsentence and turned to face her, his words hanging in the balance. His smile had vanished.

"If you're asking whether it might lead to us seeing each other again, I can't answer that."

"Why not?"

"There's simply too much at stake."

"And what if I ask you for just one more dance?" His piercing blue eyes bore into hers.

"Right here?" she asked.

"Right here."

She swallowed against the lump in her throat. "All right."

Silently he slipped an arm around her waist and drew her to him.

Neither noticed that the music inside had stopped.

Matt jammed his hands into his hip pockets as he ambled through the nearly empty parking lot toward his truck. The place was quiet as a tomb now. Most everyone had left over an hour ago.

"Man in the moon, bright stars above . . ." The lyrics from the song filtered through his mind. It had been a popular request and the band must've played it at least three times.

Yes, what a crazy, mixed-up night, he thought wearily. He tipped back his head as he stared up at the waning crescent moon. A wispy cloud glided by, momentarily obscuring it. From somewhere in the distance, the forlorn sound of a train echoed off the hillside, underscoring the emptiness within him.

He released a slow, ragged breath, suddenly realizing how bone weary he'd become. He'd stayed late, helped the cleanup committee sweep floors, cart tables and folding chairs back into storage rooms, then lock up. But he'd gone through the motions robotically, his mind hopelessly distracted. All he could think about was a certain auburn-haired beauty, this April Heatherton who'd walked so unexpectedly into his life. Dancing with her tonight, feeling her close to him, so warm and yielding, had left him wanting her more and more.

As he ambled past a streetlight, he struggled to make sense of his jumbled thoughts.

Sure, he'd had his motives for insisting April meet his father. No doubt, Dad could help chalk one up for their side of the clear-cutting issues. His father, Abraham Trendel Spencer, was a true gentleman, a diamond in the rough, as the old saying went—though it'd taken Matt himself years to recognize that after finally emerging from his fog of youthful rebellion.

But it was this same Abraham Spencer who also once told him, "Son, I expect before you settle down, you'll know your share of women. Sow your wild oats, if you must, but be responsible and fair. And when you finally decide you've found a real lady, the one you want to keep forever, then don't let one more day go by without bringing her to meet me."

Could April be that one? Matt wondered with new consternation. Had his motives for introducing her to his father run deeper than he'd first realized? What was there that drew him so irresistibly to her, that made him conjure up images of a home with a calico cat on the front porch, swing sets in the backyard, the sounds of children's laughter inside? Had he, on some unconscious level, already decided she was that special lady his father had been talking about?

Unlocking his four-wheel-drive pickup, he

hoisted himself onto the driver's seat and turned the key in the ignition. It was ridiculous, he decided as he revved the motor. It didn't make sense. Ever since he'd first laid eyes on her, practically all they'd done was disagree. What kind of a relationship was that?

He careened onto the main road, his thoughts spinning. Maybe he'd had no business asking April to dance with him again.

And maybe she'd had no business saying yes.

Chapter Four

April hummed softly as she strolled back from the grave, a small bucket of paint in hand. For several weeks, she'd been intending to brush a fresh coat on the weathered stakes surrounding the grave and at last now, it was done. How lovely the grave had appeared when she'd finished, she thought. Bathed in dappled sunlight, the tidy row of pristine white stakes had glimmered in the play of shadow and light. Just beyond grew bracken ferns and dainty flowered dwarf bramble interspersed with patches of velvety green moss.

Once again Orion trotted next to her, his head held high, tail wagging.

Giving in to the temptation to linger awhile longer in the cool shade of the 500-year-old forest, April decided to sit down on a tree stump near the side of the trail. She hugged her knees to her chest, thinking.

Two weeks had passed since she and Matt had met at the loggers' festival; she'd agreed to meet him for pizza tonight after the fire drill. During that time, Johnson Brothers had been busy completing a job in eastern Oregon, logging a small tract of lodgepole pine.

The date for the upcoming timber auction loomed nearer, in only a couple more weeks. Matt and his father talked as if the proposed harvest on North Creek Hill would go through without question. How could she, one single person, stop them?

As if sensing her discomfort, Orion gave a yip, then nuzzled close to April's side. She stroked his silky coat and murmured, "Oh, Orion, what ever am I going to do?" Liquid brown eyes smiled comfortingly up at her.

"I need to get busy," she concluded with a huge sigh. "Time's growing short and there's a ton of work to get done." She lunged back to her feet and continued on, mapping out a plan in her mind. First she'd have to make an appointment with the mayor of Wolf

Hollow, ask to call a town meeting, then organize a task force to begin peacefully petitioning against the proposed clearcut. Surely Donna would be willing to get involved. Perhaps Travis would also.

All that would mean opposing Matt fully now, she realized with unsettling clarity, for her hopes that they could ever agree were quickly dwindling. Yet maybe tonight she could turn that around when she told him about the grave, she decided. Somehow, she must convince him it was not only right, but crucial to do everything possible to save North Creek Hill.

Back home, she opened the backyard gate. Pausing by a patch of mint Gram had planted years ago, she set down the paint can, then pinched off a pointy leaf. She crushed it between her thumb and forefinger.

The poignant sweet fragrance brought a rush of nostalgia: sitting with Gram at the dining room table sipping mint tea, helping Grandmother ladle mint jelly into jars while the sunlight that poured through the kitchen window illuminated them like finely cut emeralds.

Ah, yes . . . life seemed so uncomplicated back then. The memories soothed her, distracting her from her irresolute thoughts.

* * *

"The temperatures continue to climb, topping 100, with no rain in the immediate forecast," droned the man on the car radio. "We now have an all-time record of fifty-seven days without rain."

Swinging her Ranger into the parking lot behind the fire station, she snapped off the radio. When would the hot weather ever end? she wondered. The fire danger in the forest was inching upward with each passing day. Already some of the more experienced volunteers had been sent to central Oregon to help battle several rapidly spreading range fires. Tonight's turnout for the Monday night drill would undoubtedly be lower than usual.

"Listen up, everyone!" Chief Sampson announced later after a short business meeting. He ran a hand through close-cropped hair, waiting for the murmur in the room to fall silent. "It's time to get on with tonight's drill. To begin, we're going to review the proper use of self-contained breathing apparatus, then take time to practice getting in and out of it. Next we'll wind up tonight's session with a water ball fight. I'm sure we'll all welcome a little cooling off—and it'll also give you new people more practice working with the hoses."

Donna, who was sitting next to April, elbowed her and whispered, "Obviously he means us."

April flashed her a smile. "Don't worry. We'll show them."

"Knowing how to use your air pack properly is your life-line when you're in a smoke filled structure," Joe Sampson was going on. "You can get yourself into a heap of trouble by putting your air pack on wrong or not maintaining a proper seal."

The chief lifted one of the packs from the table behind where he was standing and showed how to turn on the air tank, adjust the straps, and slip into it like a coat. Next he donned the black face mask.

For the next half hour, the volunteers practiced what Joe Sampson had just demonstrated. After shrugging in and out of her pack nearly a dozen times, April's confidence grew. Though the air pack *was* large and bulky, and the mask made the heat seem all the more stifling, it gave her great pride to know that someday she might save someone's life. Even the men's customary ribbing couldn't thwart her good spirits tonight.

"Hey, April," Jack Kolsinsky, a balding, twenty-year veteran said to her with a throaty chuckle, "I see you're finally getting into that air pack without worrying about messing your hair."

"Messing my hair?" April shot back with mock indignation. She crossed her arms over her chest. "Listen here, Kolsinksy. Someday when I rush in to rescue you from a fully involved house fire, you'll eat your words."

"She's right," Donna chimed in. She peered pointedly at the fringe of white hair encircling his head. "Besides, you're a fine one to talk about hair, Jack!"

A burst of laughter followed from the other volunteers who had clustered close by.

"Don't mind ol' Kolsinsky, ladies," Roy Foster, the assistant fire chief, said with a wink. "His wife has been trying to enlighten him about women of the nineties since practically the beginning of time. He's hopeless."

"Just wait till the water ball fight!" Jack retorted, grinning broadly. "Then we'll see who's enlightened and who's not."

The amicable banter continued till the water ball fight had begun. In an empty lot behind the station, a colorful fiberglass ball hung suspended on a wire cable between a pair of widespread poles.

"Count off by twos!" Chief Sampson ordered. He pointed to the farthest pole. "Team number one over there. Team two take this side. Hook your hoses into the engines and remember you'll be using a straight stream."

Three wide-eyed grade-school children with a collie on a leash wandered by to watch.

In minutes the firefighters had hooked up their hoses. Each team stood facing the other, alert and ready. Wedged between Roy Foster and Don Walker, a full-time firefighter, April fixed her attention on the ball— plus Jack Kolsinsky, who stood first in line on the opposite team.

Soon the chief was calling out the countdown. "Three, two, one, fire!"

As Roy eased open the nozzle, April felt a surge of water kick through the hose. She tightened her grip as the water arched into the air, zapped the ball, and pushed it along the cable to the opposite pole.

In seconds the ball bobbed back toward them, pushed by the icy blast of water that now cascaded over April's head. In an instant, she was drenched from head to toe.

"Come on, team two! We can do it!" she heard Donna yelling from the end of the line.

The men hollered as the ball was propelled back down the cable. Laughter exploded.

Again, the ball shot back in their direction. "Wake up, Foster!" Don called out. "They're gaining on us!"

Roy hunched his shoulders in renewed determination. Suddenly, in a last ditch effort, April's team jetted the ball all the way to the opposite pole. Everyone cheered.

"Let's do it again!" Jack yelled. "We'll show those suckers a thing or two!"

"Great idea!" Don agreed. "Can't resist a challenge, can we, team two?"

The chief nodded. "All right, one more time. Then we'll call it a night."

Later after the opposite team had won the second round, the firefighters rolled up their hoses.

Inside the garage, April and Donna wended their way past two fire engines, then ascended a flight of stairs to the women's side of the locker room.

April checked her watch. Matt was due to meet her in less than ten minutes! All evening so far, she'd managed to keep thoughts of Matt at bay, but now the reality of seeing him again was causing her stomach to somersault.

She showered and changed into the dry clothes she'd brought along with her. Then she hurried outside to stand beneath the large oak tree where they'd agreed to meet.

The minutes ticked by. Ten, fifteen. Matt didn't show. Where was he? she wondered, glancing around. The two weeks since she'd seen him had seemed eons ago. What if he'd changed his mind about tonight?

She peered at her watch again. Five more minutes—an eternity—dragged by.

Finally she spied Matt's pickup turning into the lot behind the fire station. Her heart leaped.

In no time, he was sauntering in her direction, thumbs hitched in his belt loops, wearing an irresistible grin.

"Hi, Bunny!"

"Hello, Matt."

"Sorry I'm late. I got waylaid by road construction on Highway 13."

"Not a problem." As she smiled back at him, her defenses suddenly melted like ice cream on a hot summer day. It hadn't even mattered that he'd called her "Bunny."

While they sat face-to-face in a small booth inside Mr. T's Pizza Place, munching on a vegetarian pizza, April silently rehearsed how she would begin telling Matt about the grave. Other customers drifted in and out, some picking up takeout orders, others seating themselves at nearby tables, draped with red-and-white checked cloths.

"Matt . . ."

"Hmm?" He reached across the table and squeezed her hand, then released it again.

"Remember that day when I came across you and your dad on North Creek Hill?"

"Sure. How could I forget?" His eyebrows shot up. "What about it?"

"Not far from where you saw me there's an unmarked pioneer grave." Her words came in a rush. "Over the past several years, I've talked to some of the older folks in town who remember it. They told me a pioneer woman who'd grown ill during her trip over the Oregon Trail is buried there. Of course, that's what my grandmother, who raised me, always said too. Consumption, they called it back then."

"In other words, tuberculosis."

"Uh-huh. Have you heard about the grave site?"

He shook his head. "Tell me about it."

"Though the grave is on county property, only a small number of people know about it and go there—a few of the senior citizens I just mentioned who can manage the walk, plus an occasional curious hiker." She drew in a deep, cleansing breath, trying to calm her jittery stomach. "I've been going to the grave for a long, long time. My grandmother was the person who first took me there. I never had any brothers or sisters and my grandfather died before I was born, so there was just Gram and me."

"Ah. So it sounds as if"—he hesitated as if searching for the right words—"you feel sort of a personal connection with that place in the woods."

"Yes. Very much so. The grave's not far from where we lived . . . the home where I'm still living." She bit into a slice of pizza, though she suddenly no longer felt hungry. "When I grew older and Gram felt okay about me hiking in the woods alone," she continued, "I started going to the grave by myself every chance I could get, especially in summer."

He studied her from across the table. "Isn't that . . . er . . . a little morbid?"

"No. Not at all." A smile lifted her lips as the memories wrapped around her. "It was my own private sanctuary, a place where I could be by myself, to read, write poems, gather edible mushrooms, and sometimes simply do nothing but daydream. I've never been a parent, of course, but I think most kids would give nearly anything to have what I did. The grave became even more special when I grew into a teenager and really craved my own space."

"I don't get it," he said. "I mean, I'm an only child too, and I had plenty of privacy. With only a grandmother around, who did you need to get away from?"

She shrugged. "No one, I suppose. But even as a child, I preferred to play outdoors every chance possible. And the pioneer woman's grave"—she hesitated—"it seemed as if it was my own secret, even though there were a few others who knew about it."

He traced his finger around the rim of his plate, contemplating. "So what you're saying is there's a real purpose to your private battle to save North Creek Hill."

"Yes, particularly the grave site. But I don't intend to keep it a private battle, as you put it, much longer. I'm going to raise people's awareness. I'm going to call for a task force of other citizens who want to save it too."

"You're staging a protest?" His face hardened.

"Of course not! I've already told you, that's not how I get things done."

He shoved his right arm across the table, exposing a long scar just above his wrist.

"What happened?" Her jaw dropped. Why hadn't she'd noticed it before now?

"This is what happens when certain bunny

huggers decide to get radical. A few years back, my chain saw hit the steel spike one of them put in the tree I was cutting down. It nearly cost me my entire arm. Next time it could cost me my life. God only knows our jobs are dangerous enough."

Her hand flew to her mouth. "Oh, Matt. That's terrible. . . ."

He withdrew his arm, then leaned forward slightly, bracing his elbows on the table.

"Listen, April. There's been some scuttlebutt going around. A few of the men at Johnson Brothers overheard those jerks talking the night of the dance, the ones we saw before we left to go outside."

"The loggers you said you didn't recognize?"

"Yep. But they weren't loggers. They were radical bunny huggers who crashed the party to try to stir up trouble."

"What? Are you sure?"

"Absolutely. They're part of a group called the Earth Crusaders."

She frowned. "I've heard about them."

"But I bet you haven't heard the latest," he went on. "Word has it, they're planning to blockade the Forest Service headquarters on Highway 40 near the Moose Run Watershed. Worse, they're even talking about spiking the trees there." He narrowed his gaze. "I hope you're not hiding anything from me, April. I hope you're not in cahoots with them."

"Matt! How could you say such a thing?" Her voice rose with indignation. "Listen. It appears you're getting the issues confused. That tract of land you're talking about is nearly eighty miles east of here, under Forest Service jurisdiction. There's absolutely no connection between that and North Creek Hill."

"Maybe there's no *direct* connection," he said, "but don't forget, Johnson Brothers has other logging interests in Oregon too. If these guys get their way even once, there's no telling what they'll try next."

"Well, they're certainly not going to influence what I'm planning to do," she answered hotly. "I said it before, Matt, and I'll say it again! Disorderly confrontation is not my style."

"Sorry." He heaved a sigh. "I . . . I didn't mean to sound so suspicious." He captured her hand in his again. "Please forgive me. It was idiotic. Forget I ever said that."

She met his soulful gaze, felt the tenderness in his touch. "Apology accepted. I . . . I guess I can understand how you must feel," she added hesitantly. "But please, Matt." She twisted the corner of her white paper napkin. "Please promise me one thing."

"What?"

"Go with me to the grave. Just one time, that's all I ask. I want you to see it too, perhaps even try to see it through my eyes."

"Why? What'll that accomplish? Nothing's gonna change, April. At least not as far as the logging's concerned."

"I realize that. But at least I'll have the satisfaction of knowing you were willing to see it, to try to appreciate what the pioneer woman's grave represents." She lowered her voice, looking him squarely in the face. "After all, you did tell me that you're fascinated with local history too. Here's your chance to prove it. Go with me."

He leaned back in his chair, his expression tight. "I'll make you a deal."

"What?"

"I'll do what you've asked, if you'll agree to go with me to *my* special place, the old mill-pond."

"What millpond?"

"Back about fifteen years ago, maybe a little longer, there was a busy lumber mill on the west side of North Creek Hill. It wasn't long after that, though, that the mill moved down the road a piece to where it's now located in Silton Pass."

"Oh, yes! Now I remember. But I never understood why it was moved."

"Harry Morton, the guy you saw talking with my father, decided it would be more centrally located there," Matt explained. "Harry still owns the original property though."

"So what's so special about the old millpond?"

"Dad and I have an understanding with Harry. He lets us keep a few boats there, a couple of canoes, a small motorboat for fishing. Harry says we're welcome to come on the property whenever we want, even camp out there. Why don't we head over there tonight?"

Her head reeled. "I . . . I don't think that would be such a good idea. I mean, I do love camping, but—"

"Oh, don't get me wrong!" he cut in, grinning. "I just thought going out in the canoe for a couple of hours might be a good way to cool off. That's all I had in mind."

"Scout's honor?" She sent him a dubious look.

"Absolutely."

She had to admit, it did sound pleasant. How many times had she tried to convince

Eric to go canoeing with her at nearby Simon's Lake on warm summer evenings last year?

Yes, she must've begged him five hundred times or more. But Eric had refused to give in, or even compromise. Better to head to an air-conditioned movie theater instead, he'd always insist. The only outdoor scenes he was interested in were those on the big screen.

"April?" Matt's voice pulled her from her memories.

"Yes?"

He winked. "What's the matter? You afraid of getting bit by a little mosquito or something?"

She laughed in spite of herself. "As many nights as I've spent camped out under the stars, Matt Spencer, bug bites are the least of my worries."

"Good! Then it's settled."

She nodded. "I guess so. We'll go there tonight. But just this once."

"I'm sorry, folks," The sound of a man's voice sliced through their conversation. "We're only five minutes from closing."

April looked up. The restaurant owner, a man by the name of Tony Armeletti, was smiling down at them.

"Oh, Miss Heatherton! I didn't realize that was you," he exclaimed, wiping his hands on his smudged apron. He sent Matt a speculative look, then flitted his gaze back to Heather. "Is there anything else I can get you folks now?"

"No thanks, Tony" she said, getting to her feet. "As always, the pizza was excellent." Quickly she introduced him to Matt, who had also stood up. "Two of Tony's children have been students of mine," she explained. "Sissy and Thomas, two of the best."

Beaming, Tony puffed out his chest. "Yes, my pride and joy." He winked. "But I owe a great deal of that to their teacher. If anyone could convince them of the importance of doing their homework, it was Miss Heatherton. She's got a real way about her, makes the kids fall right into line without the slightest whimper."

Matt grinned as he opened his wallet and tucked a generous tip—several folded dollar bills—under the corner of his plate. "Yeah, you can say that again, Tony. The lady's got a way about her. Who could disagree?"

Chapter Five

Matt opened the door of his pickup, waited for her to climb in, then hurried around to the driver's side. She inhaled the pine scent of his air freshener, mingled with the spicy aroma of his aftershave. The inside of the truck was immaculate, with seat covers of soft black leather, and the liner and dashboard a rich green vinyl.

"So when will you go with me to the grave?" she asked without preamble. "We never quite got around to that part of our agreement."

"We could go there tonight after we've come back from the millpond."

April shook her head. "I didn't mean *that* soon. Besides, nighttime wouldn't do the grave justice. I want you to see and appreciate it in the full light of day. It's beautiful, Matt. Beautiful beyond words." She hesitated for a moment, then asked, "Are you free tomorrow?"

"I'm afraid not. My father's asked me to take care of some business. There's no way I can put it off."

"Then how about the day after tomorrow? Wednesday morning?"

"That should work." The overhead glow of a streetlight illuminated the angles and planes of his handsome face, his high forehead, his perfectly formed nose.

He turned the key in the ignition, backed out of the parking lot behind the pizza restaurant, then swung onto Main Street. A strained silence hung between them as they continued through the small business district, then turned left onto the two-lane bypass that led south away from town.

"Why are you so quiet?" Matt finally spoke.

"Uh . . . what?"

"I said, why are you so quiet?"

"Oh, I . . . I was just thinking about tonight's fire drill . . . and my lesson plans for next fall," she lied. She bit her lip, wondering if he had seen through her bluff. Truth was, her mind had been filled with a kaleidoscope of uncertainties. Could this be really happening? she kept asking herself. How had she let Matt talk her into driving to the millpond tonight? Yet here they were, speeding down the straight two-lane highway that led out of town, and she'd look like a fool if she asked him to take her back.

She reached down and turned off the pager that was clipped to her leather belt. "No need for this anymore," she said matter-of-factly. "By the time we get to where we're heading, I'll be too far away to respond to any fire calls anyway."

The thought gave her pause. *One more reason why you shouldn't be doing this,* she thought guiltily. Though the volunteers normally provided the necessary backup to the paid personnel, so far that summer, she hadn't missed one call.

"How long have you been a firefighter?" Matt asked.

"Since the beginning of the summer. So far, there haven't been too many house fires," she added, "but I'm sure if this heat doesn't let up, we'll be getting more than our share of range fires."

"Occasionally Johnson Brothers helps the Forest Service with forest fires," he told her. "Though we're not trained the same way firefighters are, we often take in bulldozers and help carve out lines." Headlights from an oncoming car pierced the darkness.

"Oh, really?"

"Yes. The most recent blaze we helped fight was last summer near Wyola Falls. Man, was that baby ever something. Burned nearly a thousand acres."

"Yes, I remember." She averted her gaze, staring out the half-opened side window. *Don't let your guard slip,* she silently told herself. For a few unthinkable moments she'd almost lulled herself into believing that she and Matt were no longer at odds about the proposed logging. But they were, pure and simple, and as he'd pointed out earlier, nothing could change that.

Yet the night was beautiful—and so was being here with Matt. She caught the scent of the cooling earth, saw the dusky outlines of the rolling hills peppered with dark trees. Overhead a canopy of stars illuminated the heavens like tiny pulsating jewels against a velvety royal blue.

"We're almost there now," Matt announced, jolting her back from her contemplation. "We're about a mile from the canyon below Junction Peak." He negotiated a sharp left, then steered the pickup down a narrow dirt lane.

"I've backpacked to the top of the peak on the east side, opposite here," she told him. "I don't think I've ever seen so many different kinds of wildflowers. Daisies, redwood sorrel, blue-pod lupine . . ."

"And from this side you can even see the coast, especially Crescent Beach, plus the long stretch south of it," he put in. "The view is really something."

She rolled down the window farther and drank in the night sounds. Frogs croaked. From somewhere in the distance, a dog barked. The smell of dust tickled April's nostrils as they slowed to cross railroad tracks, then parked near an open field.

Soon they were meandering through knee-high wild grass while the moonlight enveloped them in its opalescent glow. Approaching a trailhead, they took it, then plunged deeper into the forest.

"Sorry I didn't bring a flashlight," Matt said, stopping to wait for her. He offered his hand momentarily as they climbed over a fallen tree that had blocked the path.

"No problem. The moon's still plenty bright." She paused to look around, bracing her hands on her hips. Ahead, the trail opened onto a wide clearing and beyond that emerged the millpond. "It's so peaceful here," she breathed. "So quiet." Ripples caught beams of moonlight. Through the treetops the Milky Way splashed its gossamer pathway across the inky blue heavens.

"Yes, it's pretty spectacular all right," Matt agreed. He was standing close. Much too close. She could feel his shoulder brushing hers, hear his gentle breathing.

"So where's the dock?"

"Straight ahead." He pointed. "About a quarter of a mile or so. The stars will be even more impressive once we paddle out to the middle of the lake where the trees can't block our view."

"Sounds like you've been here at night before," she said, slanting him a look. "And surely not to go fishing, at least not this late at night." She wasn't sure why the thought of him sharing a romantic evening under the moon and stars with someone else bothered her so, but suddenly it did.

He didn't answer, but only offered her an unreadable smile.

In no time they'd continued picking their way down the now pencil-thin trail. Clumps of salal on either side slapped at April's ankles. Beneath the soles of her athletic shoes, the ground felt hard and lumpy. A bat darted, a small zigzagging ink spot against the moonlit sky.

At last they came to the sandy shoreline, edged with lily pads.

"Go ahead and climb in," Matt said, indicating the nearest canoe. Its shiny wood surface glinted in the moonlight. "You paddle at the bow. I'll take over the stern." He chuckled. "You do know how to swim, don't you?"

"Of course!" she replied indignantly. "But let me sit at the stern. I want to steer."

"All right." His voice reflected his wry amusement. "Anything to keep the lady happy."

After Matt had taken his position at the bow, April climbed in behind him, at the same time shoving off.

The paddled in unison, noiselessly, with an even sweeping motion as they glided through the lily pads away from the shore.

Punctuating the silence were the sounds of nocturnal creatures: muskrats gnawing, beavers slapping their flippers near the sides of the canoe. The air was still warm, humid, and balmy. Long shadows lay across the water, contrasting the whitewash of the moon.

As they moved on, April couldn't help noticing Matt's rippling biceps, his T-shirt straining across his broad back. Poking beneath the back of his baseball cap was a rim of thick hair with a slight curl at the ends, a trifle longer than when she'd last seen him. A small shiver of awareness zipped through her. He was so incredibly masculine, his nearness pulverizing.

Farther out April could see that the pond was much larger than she'd expected. Near the middle was an elongated island, its banks laced with cattails and reeds.

They stopped paddling for a while and simply sat, neither speaking. The soft lapping of the water, the gentle rocking of the canoe, was all too mesmerizing.

And too romantic.

"Hungry?" Matt asked. "I've got some trail mix and cookies in my pack." He jerked his head toward the bottom of the canoe, where he'd tossed not only a small backpack, but the two windbreakers he'd retrieved from the back of his pickup.

"Hmm, a snack sounds good right now." At the pizza restaurant, she'd barely eaten one full slice.

"Let's cross over to this side of the island," he suggested. "There's a rocky beach there, a good spot to rest."

A few minutes later they arrived. Matt

held the sides of the canoe while moving forward in a low crouch. Next he climbed out and pulled the canoe toward him onto the shore, steadying the bow between his knees.

They picked their way over the pebbles and washed-up tree trunks until they'd at last found a large broad rock where they both sat down.

"Are you wearing a bathing suit beneath your clothes?" Matt asked. His gaze roved appreciatively over her.

"No."

He grinned all the more, then exclaimed in feigned surprise, "Oh, darn! And wouldn't you know it, I forgot my swimmin' trunks too. Well, in that case, the best way to cool off will be to go skinny-dipping. There's a nice secluded—"

"No way, Jose." She sent him an answering grin, at the same time refusing to let him get the best of her.

"No way!" He slapped his palm against the side of his thigh and chuckled. "Can you beat that? I bring the lady all the way here and she refuses to go skinny-dipping. Oh well, like I said earlier, we can always eat." He started digging through his pack.

"Yes, and you *also* said," she reminded him

levelly, "all you wanted tonight was to do a little canoeing."

"So I did." He looked up and winked. "What do you think?" he went on, handing her a packet of trail mix.

"About what?"

"About the millpond." His voice had turned serious.

"It's absolutely beautiful here," she answered. She tipped back her head for a few moments and peered heavenward before continuing. "I can't remember the last time when I've seen the Milky Way look so dazzling. The dust lanes . . . the star clusters . . . it's almost like something out of a *Star Wars* movie." She sighed a deep sigh of contentment. "I'll never grow tired of gazing up at the sky on a night like this."

"Me too." He pointed south. "Look. An astronomer friend of mine once told me that what you're seeing there is the very center of our galaxy."

"Wow! Imagine staring into the middle of something so huge, so incomprehensible."

"Yeah. My thoughts too," he said, following her gaze.

She swallowed against the lump that had unexpectedly formed at the base of her throat. "When I was a little girl, Gram—

Grandmother—and I used to sit outside on warm summer evenings much like tonight and gaze up at the stars. She used to tell me some of the old stories that her best friend Star Dancer, who was a Klamath Indian, taught her. Old Indian tales about creation, the sun and the moon, and some of the better-known constellations.

"Is this the grandmother you said raised you?" He bit into a chocolate cookie, then turned again to wait for her reply.

"Yes. Gram was my mother's mother," she answered between bites of trail mix. "My parents died in a motorcycle accident when I was only two."

"Ah, April. How sad for you . . ."

"Sad, yes. But at the same time I was very fortunate to have Gram in my life."

Blinking back tears, she told him more about her grandmother's love and reverence for the natural earth, and how she'd made sure to instill those very values into her only grandchild. "Gram also used to say that the Milky Way was scattered there by the angels, a stairway to heaven. Now that Gram's gone—she passed on shortly after my freshman year in college—I often go outside on clear nights and look up at the stars. I think about what she told me and take great comfort in that, knowing she's probably some-where up there smiling down at me." She grew silent for a long moment. "Matt?"

"Hmm?"

"Where's your mother? Your dad men-tioned her briefly that night at the dance, but you never have."

He wadded up his empty wrapper and tossed it into his open pack. "She died too. Stomach cancer. I was only eleven, just get-ting ready to start junior high school, a vul-nerable age."

"Oh . . . I'm sorry."

"After she died, for too many years I'm afraid, I rebelled," he went on, his voice thick. "I was confused and bitter. I even blamed my-self for the fact that she got sick and passed on, though I later came to recognize there was really no good reason for my guilt. Even-tually I got mixed up with the wrong crowd, lost all interest in school."

"Hmm . . . not uncommon these days, un-fortunately."

"Yes." He stared down at the back of his hands. "Luckily I didn't get into any serious trouble with the law," he continued quietly. "There were just a few minor traffic viola-tions, stuff like that. Still, my studies did suf-fer tremendously. And I'm sure all the things we *did* do—sneaking out past curfew, smoking cigarettes behind Grant's Farm and Feed—didn't make raising me any easier for my poor old dad."

Despite the tenor of their conversation, April laughed. "No wonder he seems a saint."

"Yes." The wind tunneled through Matt's hair as he turned to face her, a smile hovering on the edges of his mouth. "I'm afraid I'm probably responsible for his every gray hair."

Their eyes caught and held.

"So then what happened?" she asked. "I mean, your grades couldn't have been all that bad given the fact you went on to college."

"Middle of my senior year, I finally came to my senses and broke away from the crowd. It was a good thing too. Some of my old buddies went on to more serious offenses; one even ended up in jail for a year." He rubbed the back of his neck. "Luckily I managed to get back on the honor roll. That, and fairly decent SAT scores saved me."

"So . . . so was there some reason for your sudden turnaround?"

"Yep. It was all because of a high-school history teacher who was a lot like you. Her name was Mrs. Destler. Dedicated. Pretty. And most of all, she took a real interest in me. She spent extra time after school, helping with my studies, encouraging me to believe in myself, getting me to talk about my feelings. Finally I realized I didn't need the crowd to lean on. I . . . I guess, Mrs. Destler sort of made up for the mother I'd lost."

"Oh, Matt. That's such a lovely story. I only wish that someday I might help be able to make a difference in my students' lives too." His frank honesty had touched her deeply.

In fact, they'd both let down their pretenses, she realized with a jolt.

"I bet you *have* made a difference," Matt said, draping an arm over her shoulder and pulling her closer. He smiled again, revealing the dimple in his chin. "After all, didn't you hear what Tony was saying about you at the pizza restaurant tonight?" His deep, flawlessly modulated tone mesmerized her. "And who knows? Maybe someday some grown-up kid like me will be saying the same terrific things about you. He'll be talking about you to some gorgeous woman beneath a starry sky just like this one."

"Oh, Matt . . ." She leaned her head on his shoulder and sighed.

He stroked back her hair, placed his hand against her neck, then turned her to face him. In the space of a heartbeat, his mouth was crushing down on hers.

She reached up and, linking her arms around his broad neck, hungrily answered his embrace. His lips were warm, full, and searching, his magnetism overpowering. She could feel her heart hammering. She could feel his too.

Suddenly everything about her seemed to give way, as if she were plummeting down an endless black hole, lost in his strength, the wonder of him. The kiss played on and on.

Time meant nothing.

It was nearly five. April hadn't slept all night. Wrapping her bathrobe around her, cinching the tie tightly, she padded down the hall toward the telephone in the front foyer.

She needed to call Matt and tell him she'd changed her mind about Wednesday morning. Even though she'd been counting on this opportunity to take him to the grave site, she knew now she'd only be tempting fate by seeing him again.

Last night, thank goodness, she'd at least had the good sense to call an abrupt halt to their kissing. What a romantic ninny she'd been. Hadn't she learned her lesson in love the first time when she'd so recklessly given her heart to Eric? How close she'd come to making that same, fatal mistake again.

But now it was time to get back on track. There was work to do, a lot of work. She needed to keep a clear head without images of Matt Spencer always haunting her, constantly reminding that every letter she wrote, every phone call she made, she'd be only widening the chasm that already existed between them.

Her hands trembled as she lifted the receiver. She glanced at the grandfather clock on the other side of the foyer, her courage faltering. What if she awakened him from a sound sleep? No matter. Loggers were typically early risers anyway. Besides, all she'd have to do was talk quickly, get it over with, and say good-bye.

Her heart pounded as she began punching in his number. Her stomach twisted into a cold, tight knot. Instantly she stopped, her hand frozen in midair.

She couldn't go through with it. No, she simply could not.

Back home, in the silence of his bedroom, Matt tossed and turned. Sleep had been an impossibility. The night had dragged on and now the first gray light of dawn was stealing through his partially closed mini-blinds.

He peered at his digital clock on the nightstand. Five-fifteen, the illuminated red numbers read. Heck! He might as well just get up.

What had gotten into him, kissing April last night as if there were no tomorrow? he asked himself as he rummaged through the top drawer of his bureau, trying to find a matching pair of socks.

Oh sure, in the beginning, he had intended to steal a chaste kiss or two. Who wouldn't have? But last night had been crazy. No, *she* was making him crazy. He should've known better than to have taken her to the millpond in the first place. The bottom line was, he was wrong for her and she was wrong for him. But the entire time he'd been in central Oregon, all he could do was think about her, play out in his mind what he'd say and do when he finally saw her again.

He ambled down the hall of his three-room apartment and turned into the kitchen. Yes, last night he'd played the fool in more ways than one. He should've never let down his guard and confided in her the way he had. That stuff about his mother . . . his trouble in high school . . . they were too personal, things he didn't normally share.

He gritted his teeth, nearly tripping over Ramos, his calico cat, who'd been curled up by the kitchen door. Maybe it'd been because of those stupid stars overhead, he thought. Or the sight of the full moon reflecting off the water. Weren't people supposed to do crazy things when the moon was full?

Well, thank God, it was the start of a brand-new day. There was work to do. Big-time work. He'd better hit the road as early as possible if he wanted to make that meeting on time at the state capital in Salem. Only yesterday Johnson Brothers learned that a bunch of environmentalists were getting together with the state officials. Dad had asked him to go represent the loggers' interests, and go he would. Yep, the company was depending on him.

He refused to turn his back on his responsibilities.

Chapter Six

The ringing telephone snapped April from her thoughts. Quickly she reached to answer it.

"April! Did I wake you?" Matt's voice boomed on the other end. "Oh, gosh! I bet I did. I'm sorry."

"No, not at all. I'm just watching the late-night news on TV."

"Sorry I'm calling so late. I've been tied up all day and half the night in these darned meetings, which are amounting to nothing but a bunch of legislative backpedaling."

"Matt, what are you talking about? I don't understand."

"I'm in Salem. At the capital."

"The what?"

"The capital! Salem."

She blinked, remembering. "This is the business you said you needed to take care of?"

"Uh . . . yeah. Sorry. I guess I forgot to give you the details last night. Anyway, a few days ago, Dad and I learned that certain environmentalists were getting together with the bigwigs here. No one was appointed to represent the loggers—so I said I'd come."

She exhaled slowly. "How much longer will you be there?"

"I'm not sure yet. Tonight's agenda was tabled till tomorrow. And God only knows how much longer beyond that."

She peered at the images on the television screen. A smiling young anchorwoman was about to sign off. "So what you're trying to say is you won't be meeting me tomorrow morning," April said. "It's off?"

"Not necessarily *off,* April. Just postponed. You do understand, don't you?" He sounded drained, completely spent.

"Of course." She didn't. Not even in the light of his apparent predicament.

"But why you?" she persisted. "Why couldn't someone else have gone instead? Your father, for instance . . ."

"Dad hasn't kept up with the latest environmental laws as thoroughly as I have. It only made sense for me to go."

"Yes, I suppose . . ." How could she argue?

"Look, April." Matt's voice sliced through her chaotic thoughts. "I don't blame you if you're ticked, but you've got to understand. Tomorrow's session starts at the crack of dawn. Obviously I can't be in two places at once and I didn't want to call you at the last minute in the morning. I've just booked a room here at a motor lodge not far from the capitol building. In a few minutes, I'm going to turn in."

She tried to sound appropriately sympathetic. "Long day, I suppose."

"Darned long."

"So . . . which side is winning the most brownie points?" she asked with forced lightness.

"Neither side. At least, not yet." He cleared his throat. "Look. We're both tired . . . and I probably shouldn't have bothered you like this. I'll call as soon as I get back. We'll talk more about it then."

She closed her eyes and drew in a deep breath. "Very well, Matt. Have a safe trip home."

*   *   *

Next morning, Wednesday, April drove to
city hall to make an appointment to meet
later in the week with Ralph Schoeller, the
mayor of Wolf Hollow. The date was set for
Friday morning at nine-thirty. Meanwhile,
as April had hoped, Donna agreed to also get
involved, and by seven that evening they
were engrossed in a flurry of preparations.

"We need to start petitioning door-to-door,"
April told her friend. "It's important to get as
many signatures as possible before I meet
with the mayor. That should prove we have
solid backing. Next I'm going to ask permission to schedule a town meeting some evening next week in the City Hall conference
room, whatever night turns out to be most
readily available."

"Will one town hall meeting be enough to
get the job done?" Donna asked dubiously.

"No, I'm sure this'll be only the first of several. The best we can hope for next week is
to present the issues, get organized, and start
forming committees."

The two were sitting across from each
other at April's kitchen table, sipping frosty
glasses of iced tea and jotting down notes on
steno pads. Sunlight filtered in through the
sheer kitchen curtain. On the other side of
the window, a hummingbird flitted in and

about a fuchsia hanging basket, the delicate blooms a profusion of magenta, lilac, and white.

"Meanwhile, as I said, we need to do a thorough canvassing," April went on. "We must also start soliciting about a dozen more people to help us."

"I know Travis will," Donna put in quickly.

"Good."

"And let's not forget his two best buddies, Noah Martinson and Bernie Turnball. Noah owns his own print shop, so when it comes time to make flyers, I bet he'll agree do it."

April nodded, tapping the eraser end of her pencil against her cheek. "There are several senior citizens who might also want to get involved, for instance Minnie Wilkes, Pearl Soot, and Mr. MacAby, the postmaster. They're what's left of the original folks who knew about the grave."

They continued that way, making one plan after the next, adding to their list and weighing the pros against the cons. April had also said she intended to write an editorial for the weekly community newspaper. Already she'd chatted briefly with the editor there, who'd reminded her the deadline was Friday at noon.

Finally, satisfied with their progress, they

moved outside to the backyard and stretched out on reclining lawn chairs, sipping more ice tea and chatting companionably.

"What's Travis doing tonight?" April asked for no particular reason, other than that she knew Donna always loved to talk about him.

"He's out golfing with Noah and Bernie." She smiled, shaking her head. "Honestly! Those three are already planning their big bachelor bash the weekend before our wedding. And I can guarantee, it won't be at any staid old country club!" Chuckling, she asked, "Oh by the way, what do you think of Travis's new look?"

"You mean his beard—and his braid?"

"Uh-huh. Definitely a far cry from the close-cropped hairstyle he wore a year ago, right?"

April smiled, nodding. "I like it—though I must confess, it still catches me by surprise every time I see him. So what's his game plan? Braid today? Dreadlocks tomorrow?"

"Who knows?" Donna laughed again. "Seriously though, I told him that anything he did with his hair was fine by me, just as long as he cut it at least collar length for the wedding. My dear old dad would absolutely refuse to give me away if Travis showed up at the church looking like Fabio."

April stared down at the lemon rinds floating in her half-empty glass of tea. "Knowing your father—who is probably the most conservative investment broker in the entire Pacific Northwest—I'd have to agree."

"But there's hope for Dad yet," Donna said, setting her glass down, then linking her hands behind her neck. "His CD collection of rap music is growing by leaps and bounds, and it's all because Travis was the one who first got him interested in it."

While Donna prattled on, April closed her eyes and smiled. She was so pleased for her best friend. She was glad Donna had found the man of her dreams, glad that Donna and Travis's future together appeared so bright.

April too anticipated their wedding at the Wolf Hollow Methodist Church in mid-January, a grandiose event with nearly five hundred guests expected, followed by a reception at a popular ranch lodge in the foothills outside of town.

Though the date was still six months away, Donna had already planned nearly every detail. She'd also asked April to be her maid of honor, and with a full and grateful heart, April had said yes.

Matt.

Unbidden, her thoughts turned to him.

Matt Spencer with his blond good looks, sparkling blue eyes, and the most dazzling smile she'd ever seen. But six months from now, what will have become of him? she wondered. Would Matt be a bittersweet memory, a fleeting summer romance that never came to fruition? She knew in an instant the answer was yes. Monday night's kisses beneath the stars had been without question a gigantic mistake.

"Mind if I help myself to more iced tea?"

April's attention snapped back. "Sure. Have all you want. It's sun tea and I made plenty. There's extra lemons on the top shelf of the fridge too."

"How about you? Ready for more?"

"No thanks."

Donna got to her feet. "Gosh, if this heat doesn't let up, I think I'll go stark raving crazy!"

"Yeah, not the best conditions for a door-to-door campaign," April agreed.

While Donna went back inside the house, April mulled over her chaotic thoughts. She too felt as if she was about to go crazy, but it definitely wasn't because of the heat. She needed to confide in Donna. She needed to talk to her right now. Yet how could she share all her crazy, mixed-up feelings, when she was at a total loss to comprehend them herself?

By sundown Thursday evening, after April and Donna had taken their final tally, two thousand citizens in Wolf Hollow—nearly half the population—had signed the petition to stop the logging on North Creek Hill. While folks voiced varying viewpoints regarding the forests, watersheds, salmon runs, and newer methods of timber harvesting, most all concurred on one major issue— the pioneer woman's grave should unequivocally be saved.

Meanwhile, April had become so engrossed in her efforts, she'd only thought about Matt briefly. Talking with Donna later Wednesday evening had helped too. While April had poured out her heart, Donna had remained silent, sagely listening more than offering advice.

Yet when April awoke early Friday morning and realized she still hadn't heard from Matt, she could no longer ignore her nagging misgivings. Undoubtedly he was still tied up in Salem, she told herself. Or perhaps he had already returned home and decided to make a clean break by not phoning.

Home! Where exactly in Silton Pass *was*

his home? she thought with a jolt. Did he still live with his father? A roommate? Did he have his own place somewhere? A house like hers, an apartment perhaps? Despite his un-expected revelations that night at the old millpond, there was so much she still didn't know about him. Maybe it was best if they *didn't* see each other anymore. . . .

She showered quickly, then dressed in a kelly green linen dress with a contrasting white vest and carefully applied only a touch of mascara and lipstick.

She breakfasted on waffles and fresh wild blueberries, prepared the final copy of her ed-itorial, then carefully placed her lists of sig-natures inside her briefcase, the one she took to school most days.

She had to admit, she was growing a trifle nervous about facing the mayor. What if he refused to give the task force an open plat-form? What if he insisted that if the logging were to come to a halt altogether, small towns like Wolf Hollow would simply shut down and die?

Glancing at her watch, her nerves stretched tight, she longed for a quick retreat to the grave site where she could center her thoughts. But there wasn't time. Her ap-pointment was less than two hours from now.

At least she could finish a few chores before she'd have to leave, she decided. Given her full agenda that day, this would probably be her only chance.

Hefting the wicker laundry basket that was piled high with the weekly wash, she carried it outside. Orion, tail wagging, greeted her at the back door.

The sun beat down, promising another record high day. The dried grass crunched beneath her sandals as she crossed the yard to the clothesline. In an effort to conserve dwindling water reserves, the county had published a recent warning, encouraging citizens to cut back on water consumption by not watering their lawns. April hadn't hesitated to comply.

Moving down the line now, hanging up first two peach-colored towels, then a set of floral sheets, April could almost hear her grandmother's voice. "Ah, nothing quite like sunshine and fresh air," she'd say on the heels of a long, satisfied sigh. "Those new-fangled dryers can't hold a match to Mother Nature. . . ." And as a child at bedtime, April would never forget slipping beneath the crisp, clean-smelling linens, thinking she was the luckiest little girl in the world as she would drift off to sleep.

"Do you always hang out the wash in your Sunday-go-meetin' clothes?"

Giving a start, she spun around.

"Matt!" How long had he been standing there watching her as she'd reveled in her memories?

"I knocked first at the front door, then noticed the side gate was open," he explained. He hunched down to give Orion a few firm pats on the side. "Hey there, old fella. Looks like we meet again—this time, I hope, under friendlier circumstances."

"This is Orion," April blurted, her heart pounding. The dog only peered up at Matt and, panting, wagged his tail a little harder.

"Orion, eh?" He chuckled. "Named after the constellation, I bet."

"Yes, the mighty hunter." She couldn't help laughing, despite the fact she was still breathless with surprise. "Maybe not appropriate anymore, since he's grown so old, but it seemed like a good idea when he I got him as a puppy." She met Matt's gaze and caught the teasing glint in his blue, blue eyes. She hadn't realized until this very moment exactly how much she had missed him.

"Well, I sure hope you're not depending on good ol' Orion to protect you against all those things that go bump in the night." Matt chuckled again. "Even though I know he's capable of a not-too-fierce growl, this morning he never even barked."

"I'm perfectly able to look out for myself, Matt Spencer," she teased him back.

"Oh, yes. I'm sure you are," he said as she reached for the next towel and clipped it to the line.

"So you got your business taken care of?" she asked, quickly changing the subject.

"Yep, wrapped up for now, but not resolved. Last night's meeting turned into a near riot—right on the steps of the capitol building."

"Oh no."

"Oh yes. It was the ugliest mess I'd ever seen."

"What happened?"

"Those darned bunny huggers were arrested for disorderly conduct and the rest of the meetings were called off till later notice."

Her stomach flip-flopped with uncertainty. Here they were, discussing the very issues that separated them, yet at the same time talking in such a detached manner, as if neither of them were directly involved.

But in reality, she *was* involved . . . more so now than ever before—and the past three days since he'd been gone had made all the difference.

Yes, she realized with lightning sharp clarity, her plans were no longer mere plans now. They were in full progress, gaining more momentum with each passing day, and the campaign, so far, had proved a huge success.

What would Matt say when she told him all that?

Chapter Seven

"You still planning on showing me the grave?" Matt asked.

"Yes, but not now . . ."

"Why not?" His lips compressed in a thin line. "I thought it was so important to you."

"It is. I haven't changed my mind," she insisted, swallowing hard. She picked up the wicker basket, then realized she was gripping the handles much too tightly. She was approaching dangerous ground, she knew. "I've got an appointment this morning with Ralph Schoeller to talk about holding a town meeting some evening next week," she explained.

"Ralph Schoeller, the mayor?"

"That's right." She felt her shoulder muscles tense. "Several of us spearheading the campaign. Donna and Travis and a couple of his buddies, for instance, plus several of the volunteers from the fire department. We've already looked into the availability of the conference room, plus about a million other details."

"So this is much more than a one man show. . . ."

"Definitely . . ." She paused to inhale deeply, promising herself she'd hold back nothing. "We've been busy knocking on doors, getting signatures. So far, nearly half the citizens have indicated their support and I have no reason to doubt there'll be more."

"Oh really?" His expression remained closed.

"Yes. Several of us are going out again this weekend to try to talk to the people who weren't home the first time. And this afternoon I'm planning to visit all the shop owners in town and ask permission to post flyers."

"Aren't you getting a little ahead of yourselves? What if Schoeller doesn't go along with it? After all, the man might frown on this kind of grassroots movement."

"Our campaign is much more than some little homespun operation, Matt Spencer, if that's what you're implying. We've also gotten endorsements from several national mainline conservation groups. Besides, I'm an optimist," she added, refusing to mention her earlier misgivings. "I know the mayor will support us."

"Well, I can see you've certainly done your homework," he said. A spark of anger flared in his eyes. "But there's something I'd like to ask."

"All right. What?"

"Have any of the people sided with the loggers?"

"Of course. Logging is the backbone of this town, just like it is in Silton Pass. And several folks have flat-out refused to sign the petition, which of course, is their right. Many of my students' fathers too are loggers—and I respect that. I . . . I'm just trying to give the citizens a new way of looking at the issues."

"And exactly what did *your* dad do for a living?" Matt asked, propping his hands on his hips. "If he had been a logger too, would you still be crusading to save the forests?"

"Most likely." The tension was so thick she could almost reach out and touch it. Yet she silently determined to hold her ground. "Judging from everything Gram told me about my parents, they would've raised me to think for myself, regardless of whatever influences they may have made on me. And getting back to your first question, my father was a professor at the university in Corvallis. Mom too."

"University profs who rode motorcycles?" He gave a derisive laugh. "That doesn't exactly fit the briefcase and tweed suit image."

"Well, think what you want, Matt, but at least they were open-minded." She faced him squarely. Why, oh why did he have to be so good-looking, even when they were arguing?

"It's one thing to be open-minded, April, and quite another thing to be double-minded. The way I see it, you can't walk on both sides of the fence. You either support the logging industry or you don't."

"But nothing is entirely black or white!" she exclaimed. There are always shades of gray." She feared she was about to lose control. But then, didn't their conversations almost always turn out this way?

Matt saw the anger written on her face, heard the frustration in her voice—and realized more fully how he had missed her these past few days. What he really wanted to do now was take her in his arms, kiss the ever-lovin' daylights out of her—not quarrel.

"So," he continued, squaring his jaw, "let's

get this settled once and for all. Are we going up to the grave or not?"

"Yes. How about tomorrow morning around nine?"

"Fine. See you then." He turned on his heel and started walking away.

"Matt! Wait!"

He halted and whirled about, his head inclined. "What?"

"I . . . I just wondered if you might be free later this evening," she stammered. She wasn't ready for him to leave just yet. At least not like this. "I could prepare a home-cooked dinner. I mean, I imagine after these past few days in Salem, you're kind of sick of restaurant meals," she added as if needing to validate her invitation.

A smile hovered at the corners of his mouth. "Now, how can I pass up an offer like that?"

Matt whistled an off-key tune as he sped down the highway. It had been worth the two-hour drive to Greensborough and back, meeting with the forestry officials there, he decided. The reforestation project near Ramult Mountain was about to begin, and the man in charge had said the department would need a ton of help. If the company

didn't win the bid on North Creek Hill,
though he was sure they would, then their
men might need to fall back on that.

He braked at the next stoplight as his
thoughts churned on. Planting new trees
might not be as profitable as harvesting
them, but at least *some* work was better than
none. Several of the loggers were talking too,
about gathering edible mushrooms in the
coastal foothills this fall and selling them on
the commercial market. Not bad money, but
a far cry from logging.

His stomach rumbled with hunger. A pizza
might hit the spot, he thought. What was
that place called in Wolf Hollow where he
and April had gone the other night? Let's see
. . . he wracked his mind. Mr. G's? Mr. T's?
Yes, that was it! Mr. T's. To his way of thinking, it was the best pizza around. It seemed
to him it had been only a few blocks up from
the fire station. Shouldn't be a problem finding it again.

In no time, he approached the turn off to
Wolf Hollow, swung right, and started cruis-
ing down Main Street. He flicked his gaze
from one side to the other. Then he spied it.
Yes, that old brick building with the big sign
out front! Already the lunch crowd was making a beeline for the front door.

After parking his pickup alongside the curb, he elbowed his way inside. The place buzzed with activity. But just as he approached the takeout counter, his eyes riveted on a small round table in the farthest corner. April! She sat, back half turned in his direction, next to some man, talking fervently.

He stared harder. Who *was* that guy anyway? Somehow he looked familiar. Matt could swear he'd seen him the night of the logger's dance. Yep, there was no mistaking his full beard and long dark braid. He was one of those Earth Crusaders who'd appeared unexpectedly, trying to stir up a heap of trouble.

Matt's head whirled as realization took hold. Heat flooded his face. What was April doing there, practically nose-to-nose with that no-good bum? Had he got word about her petition, volunteered his help? God only knew, he was probably filling her pretty head this very minute with all kinds of unsavory notions. It was bad enough she was spearheading that town meeting, but now she'd allowed herself to get bamboozled too. Peaceful campaigning, ha! Not after that dude got done with her!

Flexing a fist, Matt seethed with anger. He

struggled against the urge to strike out and take the guy down. But instead he just stood there, rooted to the ground, his head still reeling. *Steady, man. Just hold on. Don't do something you'll regret later. . . .*

Drawing in a ragged breath, he whirled and stalked back outside.

April's meeting with Ralph Schoeller that morning had proved encouragingly successful. Much to her relief, the mayor had given his unbiased support and granted the task force permission to use the city hall conference room the following Thursday evening.

Travis also agreed to cochair next week's town meeting, and he and April met shortly afterward to share an early lunch at Mr. T's Pizza while they talked about their agenda. Everything was looking good, they'd assured each other.

By late Friday afternoon, posters and flyers were displayed in every storefront window. Travis and his friends had seen to it that several hundred copies were printed and ready to go.

At a quarter to five, April drove home, all the while thinking about Matt. Luckily it was still early enough to pick a quart of blackberries, she decided. Surely Matt would enjoy a fresh pie. She planned to use the extra oven in the basement where Gram had always done her canning and at the same time keep the house cool. She would also serve chicken-fried steak complete with all the trimmings. Matt undoubtedly grew up on a "stick to the ribs" type of diet, so her usual fare of salads and light entrees would never do tonight. Yes, Gram had always said that the fastest way to a man's heart was through his stomach.

At the thought, April gave a start. She certainly wasn't trying to win Matt's heart—*was she?*

Back home, she changed into a long-sleeved T-shirt, jeans, and her hiking boots—admittedly not the coolest choice on such a hot day, but her best protection against the prickly berry vines. Then, bucket in hand, she hurried to the empty lot next door and began picking her way up the side of the knoll.

A gray-brown brush rabbit, ears erect, emerged suddenly from off to the side and stared at her with dark round eyes.

April paused, smiling. "You and all God's beautiful creatures," she murmured aloud. The graceful white-tailed deer she often spied feeding at twilight. The beavers up by the creek near the pioneer grave. The velvety blue jay . . . the thick-furred lynx . . . the sleek river otters.

What would become of them if man were allowed to continue interfering? she wondered as she had so many times in the past. The thought seized her, momentarily blotting out the delight she had first felt when she'd spotted the rabbit.

She continued on and at last crested the hill where she came to the blackberry patch. Clusters of plump berries, in varying stages of ripeness, glinted in the sunshine.

April ducked down, then reached into the tangle of vines, plucking one after the next, the crimson juices staining her fingers. She plopped a single berry into her mouth, savoring the tangy burst of flavor. She ate another, and still another as memories of summers long ago flooded over her.

She and her grandmother had often stood in that very spot, in the cool of the morning. They picked till their buckets were filled to the brim, the hot sweet smells from the blackberries wafting about them.

Often, on the way back home, they would stop to gather chamomile for tea or gaze, spellbound, at a bald eagle's nest in the top of a gigantic evergreen. Gram always talked about how the Indians believed the animals and plants had souls and how the trees in the forest possessed wisdom and healing powers. At last, before the temperatures peaked, they would hurry back to start baking their pies.

Pies! The thought pulled her back. If she didn't stop eating the berries and reminiscing like this there would be no pie tonight. She started picking in earnest now, filling the bottom of her bucket with a rhythmic plunking sound.

About a half hour later, her bucket nearly filled, she heard the shrill whine of a chain saw from a neighboring ridge.

She looked up, shading her eyes. Ah yes, the old Dawson acreage, she thought. Focusing more intently, she saw the broad, dirt-colored swath that eroded the wooded hillside—reddish brown against striations of green. What any eyesore! And that chain saw—what a grating, ominous sound!

She remembered how that very morning when she had stopped by the post office, she overheard Harry Dawson talking about the logging.

He announced to everyone within earshot, "Those high-minded environmentalists might try to poke their noses into our business, but they sure as heck can't stop us from loggin' our own private land!"

If the logging did indeed come about on North Creek Hill, would her beloved forest look equally denuded? she wondered. The auction date was almost here, only a few days after the town meeting next Thursday. Time was passing much too quickly—and she and Matt were at odds now more than ever.

She expelled a long breath as she turned to leave. She was weary of arguing with Matt. Weary of the tension that seemed to chip away at their every conversation. Tomorrow they would again confront the issues that separated them. But if she could help it, she determined, there'd be no arguements tonight.

By the time Matt arrived for dinner, April had set the table with a pale blue cloth and her best china and silver. Two white taper candles flanked a bouquet of fresh-cut zinnias. Soft rock music drifted in from her CD player in the adjacent living room. A golden crusted blackberry pie cooled on the kitchen counter. Delicious cooking smells filled the house.

Yet the troubled look on his face was a marked contrast to the romantic ambience she had tried so hard to create.

"What's wrong?" she asked quickly as she ushered him inside.

"There's something we gotta get straight, April. Right now."

"Uh . . . sure." She swallowed against the sudden lump in her throat. "What is it?"

"This morning after I left your place," he said tightly, "I decided to drive to Greensborough to talk to the guys at the forestry department. On my way back, I stopped for a pizza and saw you sitting at a table with one of those Earth Crusader guys." Suspicion, cold and glittering, flared in his eyes. "What were you doing there with him, huh?"

"Wait a minute!" Her mouth dropped open. "What are you talking about?"

"Don't play dumb." He pinned her with an unremiting stare. "I saw you, plain as day. He was one of those troublemakers who'd turned up at the logger's dance . . . and . . . and there you were, schmoozing with him. I had all I could do to keep from grabbing him by his pretty little braid and decking him right there."

"Matt! Just let me expl—"

"All your talk about peaceful solutions." He cut her off as his anger mounted. "All your talk about campaigning the right way . . . how could you let yourself fall into cahoots with those tree spikers?" His voice rose. "How could you?"

"Matt, you're terribly mistaken!"

"In a pig's eye!"

She braced her hands on her hips, her chin jutting forward. "Yes, you saw me with a guy all right—but he was not who you thought. You're right on one count. He looked familiar because you *did* meet him the night of the dance. But he's not a radical. He's Travis Lagler, Donna's fiancé."

"What?"

"That's right!"

"But that dude . . . he looked exactly like those two who weaseled their way into the dance . . . I could've sworn it."

"You're talking about the way Travis was wearing his hair? His braid? *His new look?*"

"Well . . . er, yes."

"Really, Matt! I'm surprised at you! There's certainly more than a few guys around who wear their hair long. Why, that could've been almost anybody!"

He groaned. "Oh, man. I'm sorry, April. Forgive me." He reached out, pressing her to his broad, hard chest, and simply held her. "Forgive me for being such a jerk." he murmured again against her ear.

His touch was her undoing. Fresh spirals

of awareness shivered through her. "Of course, Matt." Her heart was thudding so hard she was certain he could hear it. "Let's just forget this whole thing ever happened."

He smiled down at her, his voice husky. "Thanks. Somehow, just saying thanks seems totally inadequate. . . ."

Shrugging, she smiled back at him. "We all make mistakes sometimes." She saw that certain light in his eyes, that deliciously tormenting look that threatened to reduce her resolve to mere shreds.

"Yes, but I swear I'll never make *that* mistake again." Without another word, he'd hauled her close and covered her lips with a long, slow kiss.

They enjoyed a leisurely dinner, talking and sharing, getting to know each other better. Matt told April that he was renting a small apartment on the north end of Silton Pass where in his spare time he often did odd jobs for the landlord. He also talked about his cat, Ramos, who had wandered into his front yard about two years earlier and decided to stay.

April, in turn, told him about how she'd worked as editor of her high-school newspaper and also volunteered on weekends at the local hospital when at one time she'd considered becoming a nurse instead of a teacher. She went on too about Orion, how he'd run away one day, ending up at the very school where she taught.

And while talk flowed, on a deeper level they each wrestled with that all-too-familiar undercurrent. Talk of protesters, town meetings, timber auctions, and displaced loggers lay buried beneath their carefully guarded pleasantries.

Later, after tidying up the kitchen, they wandered outside to the front porch to linger awhile. The air was humid, balmy, a trifle cooler. The breeze had picked up, fanning the parched countryside.

"Looks like a dry east wind," Matt said, the worry in his voice evident.

She nodded. "Not good. Goodness only knows the fire danger is already high enough."

"I suppose you've heard, the Forest Service called a closure on all logging operations starting today. Open fires too."

"Yes, I know. I'm surprised we—" A bright spot above the northeast horizon suddenly diverted her attention. "Oh! The Pleiades. Look! Just coming up." She pointed excitedly.

"That tight cluster of twinkly stars?" he asked, following her gaze.

"Yes, they always remind me of diamonds against a backdrop of navy blue velvet. There's an old fable that says they were once seven Indian children who disobeyed their elders. As punishment, they were cast high in the heavens, where they can still be seen, banded together, dancing in the sky. Of all the stories Gram used to tell me, that one's still my favorite."

He chuckled, a deep rumbling sound; then, draping an arm across her shoulder, he pulled her close. "And I have a favorite too."

"A favorite star story?"

"No, a favorite gal—with stars in her eyes."

"Oh really?" she quipped, reveling in his nearness.

"Yeah, really."

In the space of a heartbeat, he'd taken her in his arms and once again kissed her soundly. Then, with an effort that nearly tore him in two, he said good night and hurried across the front yard to his pickup.

Two thirty-three. Matt glanced down at his illuminated digital watch as he unlocked the front door of his apartment. Flicking on the light switch, he tossed his car keys onto the table and exhaled slowly. It was late, darned late—but he was too wired to sleep.

A vision of April flashed in his mind, a picture of a lovely lady in a white sundress waving to him as he'd backed out of her driveway. The rising breeze had whipped the dress about her, revealing her trim hips, her shapely legs. And her lips, her kiss, were enough to drive a man insane. He could almost still feel her warmth against him, all soft and yielding, smell the faint scent of her lily-of-the-valley perfume.

He glanced about the cluttered front room. Ramos was dozing on the dirty shirt he'd tossed across the back of the couch. A couple empty beer cans were perched on top of his CD player, and the empty carton from a microwave dinner still sat, wrapper and all, on top of the coffee table. His boots, caked with mud, were kicked beneath the TV tray in front of his worn leather chair.

Ramos yawned and peered at him through amber slit eyes, as if asking what had taken him so long. Why had he left her, the most fastidious of cats, in such utter disarray?

"Okay, okay, don't glare at me," he muttered. "So the place is a mess. But I was in a hurry, right? A gentleman doesn't keep a lady waiting. Besides, you realize how many days I've been eating restaurant grub? April and I might not agree about much, but she was right about one thing. That home-cooked meal really hit the spot."

He began moving in a circle about the room, sweeping cracker crumbs off the table onto a newspaper and retrieving the empty beer cans. If he was ever going to invite April over to *his* place for dinner, he'd better get his act together. After her elegant candle-light dinner, complete with her best linen and china, she'd surely turn and run the other away—or worse, take pity on him—if she ever saw this.

But wait a minute! What was he thinking? He gave his head a quick shake, telling himself it was time to get real. Just because they'd agreed to one dinner together didn't necessarily mean there'd be more such occasions.

Chapter Eight

"Mornin'," Matt said at April's front door. "Ready to go?" His rugged masculine form nearly eclipsed the rectangle of morning sunlight streaming in from behind him.

Her heart raced as she opened the door wider. "Yes, almost. I was just snapping the green beans I picked a little while ago. I'll put them away and finish later."

He stepped inside. "Take your time."

"Care for some coffee?" she asked.

"No thanks. I'm all coffeed out." He inclined his head, allowing a suggestive smile to hover on the corners of his mouth. "But I might take you up on some leftover pie."

"Sorry. I fed the last few pieces to Orion after you left last night," she teased.

"Well, in that case, I guess I'll just have to settle for a kiss," he tossed back, capturing her in his arms. Eagerly his lips came down on hers. Despite all her best intentions, she felt herself melting into his embrace.

"Hmmm, much better than blackberry pie any day," he growled after they'd stopped kissing. He traced his index finger down her cheek, then started to draw her close again.

"I lied," she told him coyly, gently pushing him away.

"What?"

"I lied. You can have all the pie you want after we come back from North Creek Hill *if* you promise to cut this out." She slanted him a wry smile. "We've got business to get down to this morning, Matt Spencer, and time's a-wastin'."

"I must say, woman, you drive a hard bargain. Making me choose blackberry pie over kisses is enough to drive a man insane."

And your walking into my life and sweeping me off my feet is nearly driving me *insane,* came her silent reply.

A short while later they started out, threading their way through the filbert grove, then moving farther up North Creek Hill.

Soon they came to the open meadow where April paused to pick black-eyed Susans. "I always stop here first to get flowers for the grave," she told Matt as she snipped the woody stems with the blade of her pocket-knife. The air felt hot and dry. Yellow and brown blossoms, intermingled with clusters of dainty red columbine, nodded in the slightest breeze. A bright orange butterfly with velvety black spots lit on a tuft of wild grass, then flitted off.

Matt merely stood by watching, silent, enthralled with her graceful movements, her near reverence.

And what a far cry from his usual treks through the woods, he thought. Somehow today the varied greens of the forest seemed greener, richer, the sounds more alive. Above all, he was sharing it with the most beautiful woman he had ever known. The others in his life had always lived in the fast track and liked plenty of action; come to think of it, so had he.

So what did this mean? What was he doing on this idyllic summer morning with a woman who loved picking wild daisies and stopping to watch the birds?

As they continued on, he reached out to take her hand. At last, they plunged deeper into the old-growth forest. Fir needles cushioned their footfalls. The scent was sweet and earthy, and the coolness was a welcoming relief. The soft sounds of the babbling creek grew louder as they approached the grave site.

Wordlessly she hunkered down, lifted the mason jar filled with last week's daisies—now withered and brown—and tossed them into the underbrush. Next she went to the creek, filled the jar with the icy water, and carefully poked the freshly cut stems inside. At last she placed the bouquet next to the three-cornered stone.

"So this is it," she said finally, her tone hushed. "This is the unmarked grave of the pioneer woman." The undulating play of shadow and light gave the grave site an almost mystical quality, an indescribable serenity.

"It's awesome," Matt murmured sincerely. He wrapped his arm around her and drew her close. "I'm not sure how Dad and I missed seeing it that day we were up here, checking things out."

April glanced up at him. "Every time I come here, I think about the pioneer woman, whoever she might've been. I wonder whether she had children, and how many, and about all the dangers she might've faced trying to protect them. I wonder about her husband and what he was like. What prompted them to make the journey in the first place."

"Yes, I guess one can't help but wonder," Matt conceded, thinking back to his own family photos in the pioneer museum.

A faint smile formed on her lips. "I also think about how pleased she would be, knowing how hard I'm fighting to save her resting place in the forest."

"She's dead, April," he said with blunt directness. "She's been dead for a long, long time. No one even knows for sure who she was. What difference does it make anymore?"

"But can't you see?" she said. "It doesn't matter who she was. What matters are the ideals she represents."

"Ideals?"

"Yes. It must've taken stamina and courage to travel all that way, leave everything behind that was comfortable and secure. Then too, the pioneer women were always intrigued by the unmarked graves they encountered along the way. Many before them had buried babies, young children. We must honor their lives, their sacrifices."

"Ah, spoken like a true history teacher," he said with a teasing grin.

"But it's true, Matt," she insisted. "Don't forget, some of your ancestors may have traveled the Oregon Trail too."

He sobered. "I can't argue with that."

"After next week's town meeting," she went on, "I expect that a lot more people will start coming here to see the grave for themselves."

"Isn't that going to spoil things for you? I mean, this'll no longer be your own retreat, April."

"True. But it's worth it, especially if in the long run, it means saving the grave." She exhaled slowly. "Besides, I'm ready to share it now. Something so wonderful *should* be shared."

They stood there for a measureless moment simply peering down at it. The quiet stretched between them.

"Matt?" She broke the silence.

"Hmm?"

"Has there ever been anyone special in your life?" She wasn't sure why she'd chosen that moment to ask, but now that she had, it seemed somehow fitting.

"I've known plenty of women." He shrugged indifferently. "And I've had my share of good times too, but that's about it." He turned to her. "How about you?"

"I've dated some."

"And?" His gaze held hers. "Was there anyone special for you?"

"Yes." She hesitated. "His name was Eric. Eric Mendelson."

"Tell me about him."

"Why?"

"No particular reason. I just want to know."

She swallowed against the catch in her throat and debated. What would it hurt confiding in Matt?

"All right," she ventured. "I met Eric about a year ago while we were each attending summer school at the university."

"Ah, the proverbial summer romance." A smile played at the corners of his mouth. "Here today. Gone tomorrow."

"Yes. A big mistake. I guess, it was never meant to be." *Just like our romance,* she reminded herself. "I was completing some graduate courses and Eric had taken a leave from his job at Arrowtek Computers," she went on, pulling her thoughts back in line. "I fell for him hard. It was love at first sight.

But at the same time, looking back now, I have to admit I was in denial." She stared down at the daisies, avoiding his eyes.

"Denial about what?"

"I didn't want to face up to the fact we shared too little in common to keep our relationship going."

"Aha! I get it now!" he joked. "Good old Mendelson didn't like trees, eh?"

She couldn't help smiling a little at Matt's last comment. "Actually, Eric's idea of the perfect weekend was attending computer trade shows, spending hours on the Internet, and upgrading his software." She waved one hand in the air. "Oh, don't get me wrong. I have a computer at home too, and I'm always glad for my students to learn all they can about them."

"But you wanted to go for hikes in the woods and canoe trips on the lake," Matt supplied evenly.

"Uh-huh." She bit her lower lip before going on. "Though Eric made a halfhearted attempt at trying to meet me half way, in the end we never could compromise. Most of the time I ended up going off into the hills by myself while he sat home practically glued to his computer."

"What a fool . . ." Matt offset his jaw,

righted it again, and added, "That man was an all-time loser."

"But that's only the half of it . . ."

"There's more?"

"Yes." She closed her eyes for a moment before finding the courage to continue. "One day Eric suddenly told me he found someone more compatible. He and some woman had been exchanging e-mail for only a short time. Then they agreed on a place to meet in person, and according to Eric, that's all it took to make up his mind."

"And so it was over . . . for Eric and you. He sailed off into the blue with Miss E-mail, and left you in the wake."

"Exactly."

Matt hesitated, but only for a moment. "You're not still in love with him, are you?"

"No. It's over. Completely. What's more, I never intend to fall in love with anyone again. It's simply not worth it." She forced herself to look at him squarely, nearly hypnotized by the burning quality in the depth of his eyes.

"You've made up you mind forever? Just like that?"

"Yes, now that—" A high-pitched beeping sound cut her off. "Hold on!" She snatched her pager from her belt loop and peered down at the message flashing on the small gray screen. "Report of a field fire on the south approach to Junction Peak."

"Oh no!" April cried. "Junction Peak! Isn't that near the old millpond?"

His face turned ashen. "Uh-huh. Next ridge over."

"I've got to go, Matt! Right now!"

"Wait!" He tugged on her hand. Let's see if we can get a quick look at it from the top of the hill!"

"All right. But we've got to hurry!"

Soon they arrived, breathless, hearts pounding. The landscape to the west revealed an open expanse of ridgelines and horizon, tainted by an ominous plume of orange-red smoke billowing into the sky.

"Field fire, my eye!" Matt ground out. "That's a forest fire—no doubt about it."

April clutched the sides of the rear jump seat where she was sitting atop the fire truck. The wail of the siren pierced the air. Thank goodness, they were on their way! She and Matt had parted quickly, and in less than ten minutes she had driven to the fire station and shrugged hurriedly into her turnouts.

"Man alive! Look at that baby!" Jack Kolsinsky's anxious shouts, barely audible now from the jump seat opposite her, competed with the noise of the engine.

Her hands grew clammy. The red glow in the late-morning sky had mushroomed higher. Though the message on the pager had been partly incorrect, there was indeed no mistake about the fire's location. Already it had consumed a large portion of Junction Peak.

A picture of Matt and herself rowing under the stars nudged her memory, but she quickly pushed it away. *Oh, please God,* she silently prayed. *Please don't let the fire spread. Please don't allow it to take the pioneer woman's grave. Not after all our hard work, the petitions, the appointments . . . we've accomplished so much in so short a time. Just give us a chance to finish what we've started. . . ."*

The fire truck wheeled around a corner, gears grinding, then raced on through the narrow streets. Rows of silvery barked alders, like soldiers standing at alert, whizzed by as the siren continued to scream out its warning.

Asphalt highway gave way to gravel road, and before long they were twisting their way closer to the base of the canyon, across the railroad tracks, down another rutted dirt

road. Finally they came to an abrupt stop behind two tankers from a neighboring rural
fire department.

April unsnapped her seat belt and scrambled down alongside Donna, who'd been rid-
ing in the front seat. Joe Kennedy, the
section supervisor, held up his hand, prepar-
ing to call them together. In the background,
the static of radios punctuated the frenzied
shouts of the firefighters.

"Number off in threes!" Joe shouted.
"You'll need to work in teams to begin trail-
ing the fire. If you're still here after we get
the blaze under control, be ready for the mop-
up. The Forest Service and neighboring fire
departments are manning the lower end of
the south slope where it's giving us the most
trouble. Right now, we estimate there's over
two hundred acres burning."

A funnel of wind roared as small pieces of
searing debris showered the hillside. April
struggled to fix her attention on Joe Kennedy's instructions, but her anxious thoughts
kept getting in the way. Those angry, hot,
licking flames . . . *Please God*, she prayed
again. *Please don't let the fire take North
Creek Hill.*

"If you need to refill your canteens, there
are five-gallon jugs on all the fire lines," the

supervisor continued. He jerked his head to the staging area not far from the fire trucks. "A first-aid person is standing close by, so if you become sick or injured, be sure to let someone know."

Overhead a helicopter hovered, showering water over the thirsty land. The whir of its blades grew louder as it lowered over the pond, dipping its cable-suspended bucket for more water.

"We need an army of helicopters," Jack murmured, his voice tinged with discouragement.

April nodded. "I heard Kennedy say the Forest Service would like to bring in some small airplanes too, but the warm air mass overhead is making it too risky."

The firefighters scattered to their appointed positions. Jack, Donna, and April began hacking away at the duff carpeting the forest. While Jack, in the lead, scratched through the top layers with a shovel, April followed close behind, scruffing away more.

Rivulets of sweat trickled down her face. The heat seemed suffocating, heavy with smoke, the odors of the burning forest. She glanced over at Donna, who was flinging aside the broken turf so that nothing but bare soil lay exposed. Her face was grim with concentration.

Tediously the hours wore on and on. With each passing moment, the heat grew more stifling. The flaming sun, hanging low in the west, mingled with the gray pall of smoke, painting the western sky with deeper hues of orange and mauve. Blackened trees with spidery, knarled branches stood in stark contrast.

Darkness fell. Wearily April trudged behind Jack, the light from her headlamp bobbing before her. The shouts of the other firefighters rang in her ears. Sparks sizzled and ignited tuffs of dried grass more quickly than the men could manage to the beat the flames out. The sparks rained down harder. The shovels thumped in a frenzied crescendo.

Doggedly they trudged on to the southeast end of the canyon, leaving behind the flame-engulfed boat ramp at the old millpond. Darkness pressed in from everywhere, darkness so heavy and oppressive she felt as if she were suffocating. "Oh, dear Lord in heaven," she whispered. "When will I ever see the stars again?"

Tears—bearing no connection with the smoke and the heat—stung her eyes. *Poor Matt. Poor, poor Matt,* she thought. The millpond was clearly his special place in the forest, just as the pioneer woman's grave was hers. What was more, part of his very livelihood was going up in flames. Even if North Creek Hill would in the end be spared, she couldn't help sharing his loss.

More smoke billowed, making the air even heavier, oppressive. April's lungs burned with each new breath.

"Those east winds have been blowing for almost twenty-four hours straight," she heard someone holler. "With this downcanyon wind, she'll be crowning in no time!"

April stopped working and lifted her gaze. The fire was rapidly raging up the steep hillside. Would it ever be contained? The air held an ominous foreboding as the rumble of the winds grew louder, like a huge roaring monster lashing out its fury.

Her clothes, damp and clammy from perspiration, clung to her. Her face felt gritty, the smell of smoke hung in her nostrils. Quickly she pushed back her grimy shirtsleeve and peered down at her illuminated digital watch. Eleven twenty-five! It couldn't be possible. She'd lost all sense of time.

She looked back at the trails she'd helped carved out. They stretched several feet wide, stripped of anything that could possibly feed the ravaging tongues of fire. She hoped against all hope they would hold back the fire. *Please don't let the flames jump over the lines,* she thought.

With new resolve she trudged on. Jack was still directly in front of her, Donna a considerable distance ahead. Suddenly April caught sight of a flash, somewhere up high, off to the side.

A flaming tree was falling directly toward Jack Kolsinsky, but his head was bent down. "Jack!" she hollered. He didn't appear to hear her.

"Jack!" she yelled again, this time lunging forward as a surge of adrenaline coursed through her. She gripped the back of his turnouts with both hands and jerked back, but he stumbled and fell forward, taking her with him. The tree crashed down only inches away.

"Jack! Get up!"

He responded with an anguished moan.

She righted herself and in a low crouch started dragging him out of harm's way. Donna, having heard the commotion, stopped in her tracks and dashed back.

"Get away from there, you two!" she screamed. "Get away from that tree!"

"I'm not sure Jack can!" April yelled back,

sending her friend a frantic look. "I . . . It's his leg . . . broken, maybe."

"I . . . I can't move," he groaned. The glow from the blazing tree reflected on his face. His features were twisted with pain.

"Donna and I'll stand on either side of you," April called to him. "Lean on us while we help get you out. We're gonna have to get you to the first-aid station."

"A . . . all right," he stammered as they helped him stand upright, teetering.

In less than thirty minutes, April and Donna had dragged Jack back down the trail to the first-aid station, where the man in charge immediately took over. "Good chance it's fractured," the first-aider agreed, peering down at Jack's shinbone after having given him a pain pill and a sip of water. "We won't know for sure till we get an X-ray."

In no time they had helped Jack onto a stretcher and into the waiting fire truck that would transport him to the emergency room at Silton Pass General Hospital.

"Will Jack be all right?" April asked, the worry in her voice obvious.

"I'm sure he will," the man answered. "Once that leg is casted and the pain's under control, of course." He flashed them a wide grin. "Good job, ladies. Kolsinsky told me all about it."

The two women exchanged a knowing glance. Yes, all the way back out of the woods, Jack had been generous with his praise, despite his pain. Gone was the banter, the teasing and verbal sparring. Gone were the remarks about women invading the male workplace. The trio was too relieved, too humbled by the prospect of near tragedy, and with that came new camaraderie.

On their way back up the hill, April said to her friend, "Stop, Donna. I've got to rest. I guess I'm more exhausted than I realized."

"Me too," Donna agreed gratefully. "Let's sit down right here."

April sank down next to Donna in the middle of the trail. Lifting her canteen to her lips, she gulped down a long draft of water. The cold liquid slid down her parched throat, yet a wave of nausea threatened to wipe out the refreshing sensation. Closing her eyes, she held her head in her hands and waited for the feeling to pass. Darn! She just couldn't get sick.

Not here. Not now.

"You okay?" Donna asked.

"Sure. Just give me a few minutes to get my bearings again."

In silence they sat. Aching. Drained. Drenched in sweat. By now the rest of their crew had moved on well ahead. Any time now, another shift would come to take over while they tried to snatch a few precious hours of sleep back at the fire camp.

Unexpectedly April's headlamp caught movement in the shadows. She held her breath as a deer, eyes glazed with fear, edged onto the trail. It stood motionless, as if held in a trance, then bounded across an access road. With heavy heart, April envisioned all the other helpless creatures, seized by terror, fleeing for their lives. More than ever now, she understood why it felt so right to be here, helping in whatever way she could.

Soon new truckloads of firefighters poured in. Clouds of dust rose as the vehicles ground to a stop. A large, burly man with a dark beard sauntered in their direction, talking into a radio.

"There've been new developments on the fire lines," he told them. "We've just got word she's spreading rapidly, heading due south in the direction of North Creek Hill. We've called the loggers to bring in a couple of Cats. Meanwhile, report to your division supervisor immediately for further orders."

April gave a quick shake of her head, wondering whether she'd heard him correctly.

Donna sprang up, tugging at April's shoulder. "Come on. This doesn't sound good."

Nodding, April got to her feet also, but the sound of a bulldozer grinding its way up the trail stopped her in her tracks. She blinked twice. Were the loggers from Johnson Brothers? Could the driver be Matt?

The next couple of hours passed in a blur. April slung turf till her neck and shoulders ached as they'd never ached before. More flames licked the night sky. More sparks sputtered and crackled. Her hair lay matted to her head in long, wet strands. Dig, toss. Dig, toss. The rhythm of her shovel nearly hypnotized her.

Without warning new nausea struck. Tiny spots danced before her eyes. She doubled over, fighting back the knots twisting her stomach, then straightened again. Never mind. There was no time for this. She had to keep going.

"April, are you okay?" Donna shouted from alongside of her.

"I'm fine," she answered with a voice much steadier than she felt. Anxiously she peered up the trail.

Back aching, she continued on. As she tossed aside another shovelful of loose soil, dust smarted her eyes.

"Man alive! I've had it," she heard Roy Foster, the Wolf Hollow assistant fire chief, say. His face was streaked with dirt and sweat. "It's time to get some more of these new guys to take over. Let's head back to camp."

"Good idea," Donna agreed.

Before April could speak also, Donna's image began to waver. Once again a sickening sensation swirled through her. Everything was spinning, faster and faster.

Then there was nothingness.

Chapter Nine

A jumble of voices floated about April's head. The surface where she was lying felt hard and bumpy.

Struggling to open her eyes, she tried to focus on the hazy outlines before her. The light from a lantern flickered. Someone was stroking a cool moist cloth across her cheeks and forehead. "April. Wake up."

"W . . . what?"

"You fainted. Everything's going to be fine now."

She opened her eyes wider and saw Matt smiling down at her. His look was tender while at the same time filled with concern.

He began dousing the cloth with more water from his canteen.

"Matt . . . it *was* you . . . driving the bull-dozer."

"Uh-huh. You're at the first-aid station. The paramedic who checked you over said you passed out from heat exhaustion." He stroked her face again with the damp cloth.

Yes, the heat. The blinding smoke. The long, long hours. Her eyes fluttered shut as the past several hours came more sharply into focus.

"Hey. Don't go out on me again," he murmured. "There . . . that's better."

She blinked, then looked beyond Matt to two more familiar faces gazing down at her: Donna and Abraham Spencer.

"There's an ambulance on the way," her friend said soothingly. "After you passed out, I yelled for help. Matt happened to be close by and came right away. He carried you back here."

"You've got to go now . . . all of you . . . go fight the fire," she murmured. "It's burning the animals . . . the trees . . . everything. . . ."

"Don't you worry," Matt's father put in. "There's plenty of help on the lines till we get back there. We're gonna lick this baby in no time flat if it's the last thing we do."

Matt brushed back the hair from her forehead and asked, "How're you feeling?"

"Woozy . . . but a little better, I think . . ." She propped herself up on one elbow and looked about, peering through the semidarkness. She could focus more clearly now. She saw that they were inside a large canvas tent. Across from her were three empty cots. Two flaps that formed the front entryway were tied back, and through the opening she noticed someone walking, carrying a flashlight. She struggled to sit up straighter.

"Oh, no you don't," Matt insisted, gently restraining her. "You lie right back and prop your feet up on that blanket we've rolled up at the foot of the cot. The paramedic said heat exhaustion's treated a lot like shock, except we have to get you cooled off. I know several ambulance drivers in Silton Pass who go to our church. I'll see if I can ride with you back to the hospital."

"I don't need an ambulance . . . besides, I thought you said I'd be fine."

"You will—but only on one condition. No more heroics for at least the next twenty-four hours," he said with a wink. "Won't hurt to have the doc in the E.R. look you over—just to be sure." He turned to reach for a plastic cup on the small table behind him. "Here, take a sip. Just a little one."

She felt him help raise her head from beneath the pillow with one hand while with the other he held the cup to her lips.

A salty taste puckered her mouth. She made a face. "Yuck . . . couldn't you have come up with something better than that?"

He chuckled. "What did you expect? A strawberry soda or something?"

"Matt, this is no time for joking."

"All right. It's a mild salt solution. As long as you can keep it down, it will help your chances of not having to stay in the hospital overnight."

She sank back down onto the cot. In the distance, the whine of an ambulance siren mingled with the drone of the other voices in the staging area. The sirens grew louder. Soon flashing red lights reflected against the outside of the tent. In minutes the paramedics lifted her from the cot onto another, metal-framed one.

Donna squeezed her shoulder. "Hang in there, my friend. I'll be checking in soon."

"That's right, little lady," came Abraham Spencer's voice. "Now don't you go worryin' your pretty little head about one single thing.

You're in good hands . . . especially with that son of my mine ridin' along with you."

She only nodded as they loaded the metal stretcher into the back of the ambulance and latched the door shut. Matt sat down alongside of her while a paramedic rummaged through a box of emergency equipment.

As they sped away, April closed her eyes again. Thank goodness, this time they weren't sounding the siren, she thought. The movement of the ambulance, the hum of the tires, made her drowsy.

Matt's voice was firm. "Take another drink of water, April. Here . . . I'll help you."

Opening her eyes again, she shook her head. It would take too much effort and all she really wanted to do was sleep.

"Come on. You want to get better, don't you?"

Reluctantly she rose partway up, took a sip, and exhaled slowly.

"Okay, that's more like it." Again he stroked back her hair and rested his hand on her cheek.

"Don't be too concerned about getting her to drink any more," the paramedic told Matt as he uncoiled an IV line. "We'll be getting a saline solution into her veins in less than a minute."

"Matt?"

"Uh-huh."

"I . . . I just wanted to say how sorry I am about the old millpond. I know how much going there meant to you."

He shook his head and said thickly, "It's gonna take some getting used to, not having it, but I'll eventually find somewhere else . . . there are so many great places around here, you know."

"Yes." She swallowed. Her throat felt so parched and dry. "You . . . you really shouldn't go to the hospital with me like this," she murmured. "They need you back at the fire lines."

"You already said that," he reminded her, his tone infinitely patient.

She lifted her gaze to him, looking fully into his face. A weary smile washed across his features, but she knew in a heartbeat it was the most beautiful smile she'd ever seen.

And I need you, too, but I can't let you know that. . . . I love you, Matt Spencer. I love you more than you'll ever know.

He took her hand in his, grazing his thumb over her palm. "I'll get back soon—but not till I first hear what the doc in the E.R. has to say. Right now you're my number-one priority, Miss April Heatherton. I hope you know that."

The last thing she remembered before slipping back into the warm cocoon of sleep was Matt's hand still wrapped around hers.

Forget it, Spencer. Matt stared down into April's face as she slept and the ambulance whizzed down the dark highway. *It's not gonna work, and you'd better buck up and admit it.* He set his jaw. How he wanted to make her his, not just for one night, one summer—but forever.

But they were as wrong for each other as any two people could be, and the truth was becoming plainer with each passing moment. Why, only yesterday she'd told him she could never love again. *That means you too, Spencer,* he reminded himself with a swift mental kick. *She was trying to let you know where you stand, no two ways about it.*

So then why in the heck was she still hanging around?

His gut twisted now with longing, regret, and a heap of worry. She looked so helpless lying there, her dark eyelashes fringed against her pale face, her lovely auburn hair matted and tangled. The IV line was hooked up now, dripping steadily in a hypnotic fashion.

Oh, how he yearned to take her in his arms again—just like he'd held her when he carried her out of that burning inferno, but she needed to sleep, to fight the exhaustion that riddled her body.

Yes, sleep well, my darling April, he thought, clasping her hand a little more tightly. *At least for the rest of the night, we won't have to think about tomorrow.*

Late the next afternoon, April stood staring out her bedroom window. Rain drops—like transparent jewels—splashed onto the deeply veined ivy that trailed the stonewall steps, then shimmered down each pointy leaf, plopping onto the next leaves below.

The window was partially open and the lace curtains that flanked it fluttered ever so slightly. As the rain-washed breeze fanned her cheeks and forehead, she couldn't help but smile. Ah, the blessed rain. She inhaled the invigorating smells that came typically on the heels of a long drought, rain against warm asphalt, rain pelting the hard, cracked earth, beading up in plump, dusty droplets. Yes, rain straight from heaven. What a welcome relief . . .

Shortly before sunrise the forest fire at Junction Peak had been doused by the driving downpour. The rain had continued all day, saturating the smoldering forest.

Indeed, April's prayers had been answered. The pioneer woman's grave had been duly spared . . . and the work to save it from further destruction would go on.

Today at home, resting quietly as the emergency room physician had instructed, her thoughts strayed to Matt. Matt holding her hand . . . Matt coaxing her to take still one more sip of water . . . Matt smiling down at her, his blue eyes brimming with tender concern—and something else she couldn't quite figure out. The uncertainty had left her with a vague, disconcerted feeling. . . .

Yet one thing she *did* know for certain. She loved Matt. She loved him more than she had ever dreamed, more than she could have ever loved Eric. Then too, Matt's role in helping fight the fire had struck her with a new realization. They had shared a common endeavor—saving the forest—and the love she felt for him was revealed to her full measure. Yes, the walls that divided them were beginning to crumble. Surely, somehow, there had to be a way for them to work out their differences . . . if only he would love her too.

The ringing of her doorbell sliced through her reverie. She hurried to answer. It was Matt.

"How you doing?" His eyes riveted on hers.

"Come in. Come in out of the rain," she said, giving a small laugh. "I was hoping it'd be you. Isn't this the most beautiful stuff you've ever seen?"

He nodded, then closed the door behind him. Leaning against the doorjamb, he regarded her solemnly. "You been following doctor's orders? Taking it easy like he said?"

After the E.R. physician had released April, they'd caught a ride back into town with the ambulance driver, who had turned out to be Matt's landlord. Then the driver dropped them off at Johnson Brothers headquarters, and from there Matt had driven her home.

"Yes, I'm getting far more rest than I need," she answered. "Thank goodness, I managed to find the half-finished needlepoint I misplaced earlier this summer. Frankly, I've never felt better."

"That's good to hear." He shoved his hands inside the pockets of his lightweight denim jacket. "After I brought you home this morning, I drove back into town and had a talk with your department chief. He said to tell you your Ranger will be fine parked where you left it in the back lot, until whenever you're able to come get it. He also said to tell you everyone there sends their best wishes."

"Thanks for doing that." She flashed him a smile, gesturing toward the front room. "I've got a fire going in the woodstove. It's rather cozy, what with the rain and all. Can I get you something to drink?"

"No. No thanks."

He followed her into the living room.

"I'll put on the CD player and pop some corn," she went on, turning to face him. "Then we can curl up in front of the fire and just enjoy listening to the music and the rain."

"All right." His dark eyes moved fleeting over her. He hooked an arm around her waist, his lips temptingly close. "Hey," he said. "You . . . you had me kind of worried for a while, you know? It's sure a relief to see you looking so good."

She touched his cheek. "I bounce back fast, Matt Spencer. You can't keep me down for long."

"That I see." He inclined his head and allowed a lazy smile to pull at the corners of his mouth. "While we were at the first-aid station waiting for the ambulance," he continued, "I overheard how you saved one of the firemen from possibly burning to death. You're one extraordinary gal, April Heatherton. I hope you know that."

"I didn't do it alone," she told him. "Donna helped me. We were both right there, the minute Jack fell. I was the one who dragged him out of harm's way, but it took both of us to get him back to the staging area."

"Okay then. You and Donna. *Two* amazing gals." He rested his hand on her neck, his thumb moving gently back and forth over her jaw. Then, with an unfathomable tenderness that made her shudder, they kissed. She was certain she could feel his own trembling response.

"I have a suggestion," he said huskily after releasing her a long moment later. "You go sit down while I pop the corn."

She smiled up at him, then told him where she kept the microwave popcorn. A few minutes later she could hear the door of the microwave snap shut, followed by three staccato beeps as Matt set the timer. While she waited, she sat down on the Persian rug in front of the woodstove and, drawing her knees up to her chest, closed her eyes.

A tantalizing vision floated to the surface of her mind. Matt and herself. Husband and wife. Spending romantic Sunday afternoons, just like this, listening to the rain while they held each other tight. If only that vision could become a reality, she thought, opening her eyes again. If only Matt could be hers for all time. . . .

Soon he returned bearing bowls of hot buttered popcorn and two cans of soda. He sat down next to her, handed her the first bowl, then placed his off to one side. Through the opened door, they stared at the thick bed of embers that sizzled and snapped. Overhead, the rain thrummed harder.

"Fire is such an amazing thing," she said dreamily, resting her head on Matt's shoulder as he slipped his arm around her. "I mean, less than twenty-four hours ago, we regarded it an enemy, not a warm, welcoming friend like right now."

"Hmm . . . a friend and a foe," he agreed as he avoided her eyes. "Life is sometimes full of contradictions, isn't it?"

"Yes." She took a bite of popcorn. *Contradictions. Just like us,* she thought.

"Matt . . ." she ventured.

"Yes?"

"Thursday evening's meeting will be here before we know it." She hesitated, slanting him a sideways glance. "Please be there.

Please go and listen to what the citizens have to say."

"Why?" he asked, turning to look at her.

"Why not?" she countered.

His gaze hardened. "Listen, April. There's something we've got to get straight. The timber auction will be here soon also—just a half week after the town meeting. Johnson Brothers certainly won't pull out now, not when there's this many board feet of harvestable timber at stake."

"And exactly where do you plan to start clear-cutting?" she asked pointedly. "Assuming, of course, you do win the bid."

"There's a forty-acre tract on the northwest side of the hill with the least number of protected resources—fewer streams and tributaries, that sort of thing. Our company will begin harvesting there as soon as our notification of operation is approved."

"I see." A coil of fear, mingled with fresh determination, twisted inside of her. "I hope you realize, Matt," she continued, "that even after the bid's finalized, our task force won't give up." She never once faltered beneath his steady gaze. "We'll keep working as hard as we can. We'll do whatever is necessary to continue fighting for what we believe in."

An icy silence hung between them.

Matt, at last, was the first to speak. "April
. . . what exactly . . . do you want from me?"

"Your understanding . . . your cooperation
. . . maybe even your help. Many who've
signed the petition have indicated they don't
object to the logging on North Creek Hill as
long as it's done responsibly. They've also
suggested we find a way to protect the area
around the grave site itself where the
greatest density of old-growth timber grows.
To me, that seems a reasonable compromise."

The artery in his neck throbbed. "Try to see
it our way," he said, wrenching his eyes from
hers. "The proposed contract with the mill is
for the entire hundred-acre forest, not just
part of it. The pioneer woman's grave is special—that much I'll agree—but the bottom
line is, mere sentiment isn't enough. Our
men have been without full-time employ-
ment far too long. The anticipated yield will
help make up for months of slack time. It's
all or nothing, April. That's the way it must
be."

"But Matt—"

"No buts about it!" he insisted. "Stop and
think, April. Even if our company stepped
out of the picture altogether, someone else
would step in and win the contract anyway."

He sent her an incredulous expression. "You really think I can stop the logging?"

"Oh, Matt." She sighed. "Sometimes I'm not sure what to believe anymore."

"And neither do I," he confessed. "But after the forest fire, I . . . I've been mulling things over, long and hard. I've been thinking about us, about where our relationship appears to be headed. . . ." He cupped her chin in his palm and gently turned her to face him. "I want you to understand I care a lot about you. More than you'll ever know . . ."

"And I care about you, Matt. In fact, I think I—"

"Sh!" he put his finger to her lips. "No. Don't. It'll only make what I'm about to say next a thousand times more difficult." He hesitated, as if wondering how to continue. "It doesn't take a rocket scientist to figure out we're two very different people, with very different goals. But sometimes caring just isn't enough—not when we seem to keep spinning our wheels, hashing out the same old problems."

"Yes, but maybe there's a way we can finally work through that," she said softly. She longed to add that perhaps love was the answer, but something told her it was better left unsaid.

"I don't see how. It's obvious we've come to an impasse. Maybe the real problem is a matter of trust on both our parts, I can't really say. But whatever, it's getting us nowhere."

She turned away and swallowed, struggling against the sorrow that was welling up inside. At last she forced herself to look at him again. His eyes reflected his own regret. "So . . . what you're trying to say is, we shouldn't see each other anymore?" she asked in a faint voice.

"Yes," he rasped. "I guess I am. It'll be a darned sight better that way, believe me. Much better for both of us."

Chapter Ten

In a matter of minutes, they'd exchanged stilted good-byes, then parted. From inside her closed front door, she listened to his footsteps grow fainter. Then came the slam of the truck door, the rev of the engine, and the swish of wet tires as he drove away.

Hot, stinging tears pricked at the base of her throat. She blinked rapidly, promising herself she would remain strong. Yet the tears flowed freely. Who was she trying to kid? Truth was, she *had* allowed herself to fall in love again. This time, she loved with every fiber of her being. She loved Matt Spencer more than she'd ever loved before.

* * *

Matt turned onto the narrow dirt lane that led to his childhood home, the home where Abraham Spencer had continued to live nearly two decades after the death of his wife. Fatigue weighted Matt's shoulders. Every muscle ached. He'd been driving for hours . . . forever, it seemed. Just thinking . . . and driving.

He'd passed the armory, the place where he'd danced with April, where he'd first held her tight, then fallen in love with her. He'd driven by the historical museum, thought about his family photos there and the unmarked grave of the pioneer woman on North Creek Hill.

What had he done, turning away from the best thing that had ever happened to him? he wondered feverishly as he approached the end of the drive. He couldn't deny that in the beginning their attraction had been like dynamite, but that attraction had grown to something else . . . something good and pure . . . something he wanted to hold on to forever.

He spied his father's pickup parked near the maple tree where Matt's old swing still hung from a thick rope. Ah, to be a kid again, he thought, heaving a sigh. To be a kid with a mom and a dad, and not have to worry about grown-up things like love gone wrong.

Sauntering up to the front door, he noticed the porch light was already on, though it was still several hours till dark. Maybe Dad never bothered to turn it off when he'd first dragged in from the fire lines, Matt decided, at the same time wondering why it was suddenly important to fill his thoughts with such mundane details.

"Hello! Anybody home?" he called. He poked his head through the front door and went inside. The mouth-watering smells of bacon sizzling and freshly brewed coffee drifted in from the kitchen, but they failed to tempt Matt's taste buds. He hadn't felt such a dull ache in the pit of his stomach since his mother had died.

"Back here, son!" Abraham Spencer called.

Matt found his father hunched over the kitchen counter, fork in hand, beating a bowlful of eggs. "Just in time for supper," he said, sending Matt a welcoming grin. "Scrambled eggs, bacon, and toast—nothin' fancy. I'll throw in a couple more eggs and—"

"Ah, no thanks, Dad," Matt said. He collapsed onto a chair, folding his long legs beneath him and holding up one hand. "I really couldn't . . . not now."

"What? You comin' down with something? Or maybe you got just plum worn out, battlin' that blaze."

"Yeah, that's it—the fire," Matt agreed a little too quickly.

The older man gave the fork a shake against the bowl, then set it down in the sink before rambling on. "For a while I was 'fraid we were gonna have another bad one like the Tillamook Burn back in '33. I can still remember my pa and the other old-timers swappin' stories from when they lived in the loggin' camps. When Pa and the others weren't workin' in the woods, that's what they like to do best. Chew the fat and talk about the old days, especially that Tillamook Burn up near Gales Creek."

Matt nodded. "I've read about it. And heard the talk too. Two hundred and forty thousand acres gone up in smoke." He inclined his head. "Does anyone know for sure what caused *yesterday's* fire?"

"Some fool camper burnin' an illegal campfire."

Matt rocked back in his chair. "We can thank our lucky stars it was contained before we ended up losing our contract. It was heading straight to North Creek Hill, no two ways about it."

Matt's father grunted his agreement as he poured the egg mixture into a cast-iron skillet.

Contemplating, peering at the floor, Matt focused on the pale green and beige patterns in the off-white linoleum. Several seconds lapsed before he looked up again.

"Sure you ain't hungry, son?" the older man asked as he joined Matt at the round oak table, the table where Matt and his parents had shared many a meal. "As you can see, I got plenty of grub," he added.

Matt managed a smile. "Looks like you were expecting the entire fire crew and then some. Maybe I'll help myself a little later to a cup of coffee, but right now, I couldn't eat a bite."

"Suit yourself." Abraham Spencer bit into a slice of buttered toast. "By the way, how's that little lady of ours doing now? Have you checked on her?"

"She's fine. I just came from her place. But she's not 'our little lady,' and I'm warning you, Dad, you'd better make sure she never hears you calling her that again. April Heatherton is totally a nineties woman, in sort of a sentimental, old-fashioned way." He gave a rueful laugh. "I know that doesn't make much sense, but it's true."

"Huh." Abraham Spencer looked up and grinned, then washed down his next bite of toast with a mouthful of coffee. "A nineties woman. That's what they all say."

"April isn't like all the rest. I've never known anyone like her before. She . . . she's one in a million, Dad, the person you always told me I'd someday find, the one you said I should bring home to meet you when I knew the time was right." He swallowed hard, balling one hand into a fist. *And now that I've found her, I've blown it by telling her goodbye.* Matt hesitated. "Dad?"

"Yes, son?"

"Did you and Mom . . . did you always agree—on most things, anyway?"

"Now that could take all night."

Matt lifted one shoulder. "I have all the time in the world. . . ."

"Okay then." Abraham Spencer broke into a slow smile, his eyes bright with a faraway look. "Your ma and I, it seemed sometimes we came from two different planets. As I think you probably know, we met a long time ago when I was cooped up at Silton Pass General after I took a bad fall in the woods and got busted up. I was twenty, barely dry behind the ears, and your ma, who was in nurse's training, was 'bout the prettiest little thing I'd ever laid eyes on."

Matt couldn't help smiling too.

"Anyway," Abraham Spencer went on, "one thing sort of led to another and before I knew it I was marchin' her down the aisle. That's the only way she'd have it, of course. A church weddin' with all the bells and smells." His smile quickly faded as he stared hard into his coffee mug. "That was also the time she gave up her schoolin'. There were days, I think, she probably had some regrets. Maybe she wasn't cut out to be a logger's wife, but she rarely complained."

"She was happy, wasn't she, Dad?"

"Oh yes. She loved us both, and she doted on you like only a mother could. Your ma and I were both happy, but that doesn't necessarily mean we always agreed."

"Tell me about it . . ."

"Well, for starters, your ma enjoyed spendin' time in the woods. She liked to watch the birds and other small critters, not to mention her leavin' out food for the deer and scatterin' feed for the sparrows after it snowed." He reached for the pipe and tobacco he'd tucked inside his shirt pocket, filled and lit the pipe, then took a long draw. "I guess she probably was thinkin' that since she wasn't out helpin' sick folks get well, she'd take to helpin' the wildlife instead."

"Guess that makes sense," Matt agreed, drawing a silent comparison between his mother and April. Yes, teachers and nurses definitely had something in common—they both worked in "helping" professions.

"Come every spring, though, when it came time for her to put in her vegetable garden, we'd have our same old go-around," Abraham Spencer continued. "We always tried to save our squabbles till when you were off at school or with your buddies though. Your ma never wanted you to hear us disagreein'."

"Oh?"

"Yep. I kept tryin' to tell her if only she'd let me fall those firs back by the toolshed that were blockin' out the sun, she'd have a dandy spot. Soil is rich and black as coal there, yes it is—a danged sight better than that bed of clay where she always insisted on doin' her plantin'." He shook his head, the furrows in his brow deepening. "She kept sayin' it took forever for those trees to grow, not to mention the nestin' place it gave her birds. But of course when it came to us loggin' the woods, she knew full well it was our bread and butter."

"So did she ever come around to your way

of thinking?" Matt asked. "About the garden, I mean?"

"Nope," Matt's father answered. "Your ma, she just kept plantin' in that same old spot and every summer her vegetables came up pale and scrawny, starved for sunlight. But I bit my tongue and never pointed that out to her—at least not till it came time for plantin' again the next year."

"But Mom sure did make the best green tomato relish this side of the Mississippi River!" Matt pointed out.

"You can sure say that again!"

Father and son shared a chuckle.

"There's something I don't get," Matt continued, crossing his arms across his chest. "After all, fussing over taking down a few trees in the backyard isn't really *that* big a deal."

"You're right." Abraham Spencer took another drag on his pipe, then studied Matt long and hard. "It wasn't our squabbles about the trees and the birds and the garden that mattered in the end." He cleared his throat. "Only a year or so before your ma got sick, we decided that when you'd grown a little older, she'd go back to finish her schoolin'. We knew it wouldn't be easy, her drivin' every day for nearly an hour into the big city and back, not to mention you and I havin' to do the chores around the house she was accustomed to doin' herself. But she wanted to make the sacrifice and I was happy for her. That's what it's all about, Matt. Hard work and sacrifices. Lookin' out for the other guy's happiness more than your own." A shadow passed across his face. "I . . . I still sometimes can't believe she's not around anymore. Not one day goes by, I don't still think about her. . . ."

"Yes," Matt breathed, squaring his jaw. "I miss Mom too. I wish I could've known her better . . . and longer." He met his father's soulful gaze. "It sounds like the two of you had what it took. I guess I'm envious of that. I wish I could say the same for April and me."

"Hmm. You two have a little spat or something?"

"It seems we're *always* having the same little spats." Matt sighed heavily and shrugged. "You heard her that first day up on North Creek Hill, didn't you? You heard her carrying on about us cutting down the old-growth timber. Well, it's even worse now." He filled his father in on the details about the upcoming town meeting in Wolf Hollow and the pioneer woman's grave.

"You love her, son?"

"Yes, I do. All the other women . . . back in college, and here again at home . . . well, they were just for kicks, you know? But not April. I do love her. I never dreamed I could love any woman the way I love her." He paused. "I want to marry her, Dad."

"Then do what you have to. There *are* ways. Sometimes the answers are really closer than we think." Abraham Spencer leveled his son with a meaningful look. "If you really love her as you say you do, don't let her go."

"Ladies and gentlemen, on behalf of the Wolf Hollow pioneer grave task force, Travis Lagler, my cochairman, and I would like to thank you for coming here tonight." April gazed out at the sea of faces staring back at her, nearly a couple hundred, she guessed. Ralph Schoeller, the mayor, sat in the front row next to Reverend Camby, the minister of the Methodist Church. Jack Kolsinsky and several other firefighters, plus a few of the city fathers, were there also.

She and the rest of the twelve-member task force were seated up front behind a long, narrow table. Donna and Travis were positioned on either side of her.

Gesturing, she introduced each member of

the task force, then finally herself. "Since many of you here have already signed the petition," she continued, "you're already acquainted with our mission statement. But for those of you who are not, we'd like to stress that our work will be carried out in a strictly nonconfrontational manner."

Her stomach turned over at the sound of her last words. How many times had she tried to convince Matt of that? But she mustn't think about him now—no, not now or ever again.

Reigning in her thoughts, she quickly noted that a few latecomers had just entered, taking their place next to those who were standing at the back. Yes, every folding chair in the conference room was taken.

April went on to explain about the pioneer woman's grave, detailing its exact location, estimated age, and a description of the old-growth timber surrounding it. Next she told about the timber auction, only four days away, and the measures they would need to take to try to reverse it.

Travis followed with recommendations from two mainline conservation groups and made suggestions to begin forming committees.

"Our next step will be to talk with the officials at the State Historic Preservation Offices," he said. "This is where laws about historical places are explained. But before we do, I'd like to ask for a volunteer to draft a letter and request a meeting date."

"I'll be happy to do that," Reverend Camby spoke up, lumbering his feet. "As many of you folks may know, I'm Reverend Camby, pastor of the Methodist Church. I'm proud to say my kin date back to some of the earliest missionaries who helped settle Oregon. Though I, for one, have nothing against carefully managed logging, I believe the unmarked grave of the pioneer woman—and perhaps a reasonable buffer zone around it—must be preserved at all cost."

A murmur of consent and a shuffling of feet filled the room.

A petite, trim woman was the next to take the floor. Recognizing her immediately, April smiled at her in welcome. How could she forget the woman from the historical museum who had so graciously assisted her that day of the loggers' festival?

"I too cast my vote to protect the grave site," the woman proclaimed. "As a long-standing member of the Oregon Historical Society, I pledge my support in any way needed. I suggest we sponsor guided interpretive walks to North Creek Hill so we can teach folks more about the early settlers who came on the Oregon Trail."

Several more people took turns speaking. Each seemed fueled with equal determination. A biologist from the Fish and Wildlife Service presented information about endangered species and other protected resources. Two history teachers from the high school where April taught also voiced their support, and a group of junior high students told about their recent class project to help restore the salmon in North Creek.

In closing, April posed a final suggestion. "Because North Creek Hill—and most specifically the pioneer's woman's grave—is part of the Ramult County Forestry Program, I suggest we appoint a committee to speak with the county commissioner. He's the man in charge of appointing the county forester, who ultimately might prove our greatest source of help."

"Hold on! That's already been done!" a voice piped up.

Matt! April's head whirled at the sight of him elbowing his way inside. She clasped the edge of the table, feeling herself break into a cold sweat. *Get a grip, Heatherton. Don't cave in now.*

"Madam chairperson, I'm sorry I missed the first part of this meeting. May I have the floor for a moment?" he asked. His gaze locked with hers.

"Yes. Go ahead." She swallowed. Her throat felt suddenly parched. "But before doing so, state your name and affiliation, please."

"Gladly." He sent her a tight smile. "My name is Matthew Spencer. I'm employed by my father, Abraham Spencer, longtime owner of Johnson Brothers Logging in Silton Pass. You folks may or may not already know that Johnson Brothers will be among those bidding on the upcoming timber auction at North Creek Hill. I'm here this evening to inform you of some late developments."

Muted comments rippled throughout the room. Someone coughed.

"And what exactly do you mean, Mr. Spencer, that the county forester has already been contacted?" April never wavered beneath his piercing gaze as she presented the question with a strength she no longer felt.

Matt dipped his head momentarily, then glanced around the room. "Ms. Heatherton, task force, citizens of this community . . . though you're probably assuming right now

I'm here to oppose your actions, I want you to know I am not.

"I know all about the pioneer woman's grave. I've visited it too. I do understand its significance. Three days ago when I spoke with a Mr. Todd Logan, the Ramult County forester, I submitted a formal request that a ten-acre 'set aside'—a buffer zone, actually— be designated around the grave site. This morning he phoned back, granting that request. Next Monday morning, the pioneer woman's grave and that surrounding ten acres will become a protected historical site. The action will go on as planned—but I assure you, regardless of whatever company wins the bid, the buffer will remain untouched."

A burst of applause filled the room. Concerned looks gave way to ready smiles. Folks turned to those sitting on either side of them, nodding and talking.

But April sat rooted to her chair, too stunned to speak. Thank goodness, Travis lost no time winding up the rest of meeting.

The wedding took place near the grave site one morning the following June, when the forest was verdant with new life. What better way to pledge their love before God and man, the bride and groom had agreed, a love that would last for all time . . .

April, attired in a white satin dress and a shoulder-length train studded with intricate beadwork, was the picture of serene joy. She carried a bouquet of mixed white and gold daisies.

Matt had never appeared more handsome. Smiling radiantly, he was dressed in a black tuxedo with a carnation boutonniere.

While Donna, the matron of honor, stood by April's side, a beaming Abraham Spencer presented himself as Matt's best man. The only music was the sound of the birds and the babbling of nearby North Creek.

The simple ceremony, conducted by Reverend Camby, brought tears of joy to the several people who'd gathered to witness it.

"I love you so much, Matt Spencer," she murmured after the ceremony had ended, and, smiling, they turned to accept the applause from family and friends.

Matt could only capture her in his arms and kiss her again, this time with an intensity that far surpassed their brief kiss only a moment earlier after the pastor had pronounced them man and wife.

"I guess miracles really do happen, my darling," he whispered fiercely into her ear as the applause grew louder.

"You'd better believe it," she whispered back, overwhelmed by the love she saw in his eyes.

Yes, the pioneer woman's grave would be hers forever and ever. And so would Matt.